Angelina ran as fast she could to get in front of the young boy to protect him. She didn't think about what was going to happen. She didn't care about herself. All she knew was she had to save the kids; nothing else mattered to her at that moment. She shielded Jamal, and the last thing she heard was a bang.

ANGEL

Never Lose Faith

By C.C. Russell

To order additional copies of this book, contact:
Xlibris Corporation
1-888-795-4274
www.Xlibris.com
Orders@Xlibris.com
111345

DEDICATION

To my dad, Larry Campbell
(Rest in peace)

I will always take you with me in my heart. That is where you live! You taught me to never give up, never lose faith, and never question God. This book is for you and me, Dad. It's all my love and pain and creativity.

When I couldn't control what was happening in my life, I created a world that I could control. Whenever I wanted to give up on myself or started losing faith and questioning God, I wrote my heart out.

Writing this book gave me hope and helped me grieve. I hope it touches others' hearts as it is a piece of mine.

CHAPTER 1

"Hello, Ms. Heart, I am Dr. Dina Hayford. Please come in to my office. We can begin our session."

She was tall and thin, with frizzy grayish-blonde hair, that she wore in a bun. She didn't seem as old as she made herself look. She couldn't be much older than forty. She was wearing a gray suit with a purple blouse. She sat down in her office in a big black chair with a pen and a pad of paper. The room was small but classy, and it had a calming feel to it. The walls were soft-blue in color. And on the wall, by the window, sat a desk with a computer on it. Behind the desk was a shelf filled with books. All the furniture was black, and it was set up like a meeting room. There were nice big plants set out and arranged in such a way as to convey a feeling of comfort and ease to the patients.

Angelina Heart walked into the room and sat in one of the black chairs across form Dina Hayford. Angelina was a twenty-four-year-old college student attending a university in Toronto, Ontario. Angelina was about five feet- five inches tall, and had the softest and silkiest long, dark brown hair. She had a round face with a button nose and big puffy lips. She had the most captivating big brown eyes that were round in shape, and her lashes were so long it made her eyes stand out, and reflected something so pure deep inside. Yet, so much sadness could be seen in those eyes. Her beauty and stunning features were often noticed by others; but she did not even care to notice them herself.

"So, Ms. Heart, why are you here?" asked Dr. Hayford.

"The school is making all psychology students that are red flagged have psychiatric evaluations before work placement," she replied. "And please call me Angelina."

"OK, Angelina, why would you say that you are a red-flag student?" asked Dr. Hayford.

"You already know why I am here, but I guess you are going to make me tell you. I am here because the university has to make sure that I am stable, before they can let me go out into the community and work with people," Angelina responded with a hint of annoyed frustration.

"Why would the college think you could be unstable?" Dr. Hayford asked.

Angelina put her head down, feeling a surge of suppressed emotions beginning to surface. She didn't look Dina in the eyes but kept her head down, avoiding eye contact. After what felt like forever, Angelina spoke up, "You are going to make me relive every bad thing that has ever happened in my life, aren't you?

Then you are going to see my reaction and *shrink* me," Angelina said.

A single teardrop fell down on the left side of Angelina's cheek. "You want to know what has happened in my life?" she responded as her voice began to crack and she fought back more tears. "I'll tell you. It will be hard, and I will cry. But before I do, I just want you to know, Dr. Hayford, that I am not crazy. Despite everything I have been through in my life, I still have faith. Please, just give me one minute to get myself ready for this."

Angelina took a deep breath, and before she exhaled, she could feel a lump in her throat. Rubbing her hands back and forth on her jeans, she kept her head down for a few minutes; then very calmly she raised her head and looked at Dr. Hayford; their eyes met, and she began to speak: "I am ready, but you will never forget me after you hear my story!"

Angelina got up out of the chair and walked to the window and stared outside for a while, and she breathed heavily.

"I was five years old. It was November 28, a Thursday, and my mother and I were at our church. My mother was practicing for choir, she sang every week. She had such a beautiful voice, and she sang the most beautiful song I have ever heard. I remember the song, but I have never heard that song again since my mother sang it.

"We were running late. We ran as fast as we could to get to the bank before it closed. We were meeting my dad there. He worked at the bank. I remember we made it to the bank before it closed, and my mom said, 'Thank God." I will always remember those words.

"As soon as we got to the bank, I ran to my dad. I was so happy to see him. He gave me a big hug, and then I went to the playhouse. That's where I always played when we went to the bank. While I was playing, I heard screaming. When I looked out the little window of the play house to see what was happening, I saw everyone on the ground but three men with guns. One man had a big knife. These men had tattoos all over their arms. I saw my dad. He was at the counter, giving the man money. I couldn't find my mom. My eyes looked everywhere, but I couldn't see her. Then I heard sirens, and I felt my heart beating fast. I knew the policemen were going to come and take the bad men away. The man with the knife got really mad at my dad, and he kept yelling."

"What did you do? Now you're really going to pay," screamed the man.

"The man turned and that's when I saw my mom. He had her in his arms. He held a knife to her throat, and I was so scared; but I stayed hidden in the playhouse. I don't remember what happened next. People were screaming, and people were running in fear. Then I saw my mom was on the ground and there was blood everywhere. My dad was holding her, screaming. One man was holding a gun to his head, and then *bang!* It all happened so fast I didn't even comprehend what was happening, and before I understood what was going on, everything was done. I don't know why, but both my parents were dead. I remember walking over to my parents and just staring at them. Both of their eyes were open, but their eyes were empty. It was heartbreaking I could barely breathe,"

Angelina stopped talking for a minute to catch her breath. She continued to look out the window as tears ran down her face. She wrapped her arms around her body like she was giving herself a hug. She started shaking, because she was crying so hard. She turned around and walked over to the big black chair and sat down, making sure she didn't look Dina in the eye. She held her head down once again before she began talking.

"I am sorry. I haven't relived that in a long time, and I try not to think about that day when I think about my parents." Angelina said.

"That's horrible. I cannot imagine having to witness something like that," Dr. Hayford replied, almost at a complete loss for words. "So what do you think about when you think about your parents?"

"I think about my parents! But not about how they died. I think about our family dinners and playing games with my dad. I think about my mom singing to me at night. I think about how much they loved me and how much I loved them."

Tears kept falling down her face, but Angelina had calmed down enough to talk. Dina handed her a tissue.

"Angelina, do you feel you can continue? You can tell me what happened next, or we can be done for the day. It's up to you. We still have time if you want it," Dina said, looking at Angelina.

Angelina looked her in the eyes. "I am not doing this again. You can hear it all today. I can't do this again," Angelina said, shaking. She shut her eyes and went back to that horrible day. She hated that she had to talk about all the bad things in her life, but she found strength within herself to finish her story.

"There was a policewoman. She was really nice to me. She held me in her arms for a while, until my aunt Jenny came to take me home with her. Jenny was my mom's younger sister. I remember she was a mess. Her golden-brown hair was everywhere, and her almost yellow eyes had makeup running down her face. Jenny was in my bed with me all night holding and comforting me. She held on to me, and we both cried and cried. She told me that all the bad men were going to jail, so they couldn't hurt anyone else again. Jenny also told me that my mom and dad went to live in heaven with God. She said that they would be so happy there and one day I would see them again,"

"After that, life was really crazy for a long time. There was the funeral, and then they had to figure out what to do with me. I went to live with my grandma. She lived here, in Toronto," Said Angelina " I have lived here my whole life. I was with my grandma, who was my mom's mom, only for about one year. Right after my sixth birthday, my grandma had a bad fall and ended up in the hospital. I stayed with Aunt Jenny when Grandma was sick. I went to the hospital every day after school, while Jenny was at work. I would just sit and talk to Grandma and tell her how much I loved her,"

"One day, she just looked at me and took a big, deep breath, and then the machine went *beep beep beep*! That was the day my grandma died. She seemed at peace, her eyes closed, like she just went to sleep. I stayed in the room until a nurse came in and picked me up and took me to the hall. "My grandma went to heaven to be with God and my mom and dad," I told the nurse. I understood that, and in some way, I found comfort in knowing that they were all together,"

"I remember Aunt Jenny coming to get me. She was young—only twenty-one—and she had to take care of a six-year-old. So my dad's brother, John, and his wife, Eva, who also lived in Toronto helped her with me,"

"They took me all the time to help Jenny out. I lived with my aunt Jenny, and she always went out of her way to make it comfortable for me. She was the best, and I loved her so much. She was my best friend I was so lucky to have her in my life. She taught me how to read, and she would buy me any book I wanted even if they were too old for me."

"I didn't have a lot of friends growing up, because parents of kids my age that knew my parents treated me funny. And I didn't really have a lot in common with most kids my age. I didn't care about Barbie or playing dress- up. I really just liked to learn things. I hung out at my church a lot with Father Patrick, and he is still my friend to this day. He really is the only person that talked to me about my parents. He is someone that has been through everything with me.

"I lived with my aunt Jenny until I was nine. On my birthday, Aunt Jenny told me that we were going to move into my Uncle John's apartment building. He and his wife, Eva, had their own building. I was going to live with Uncle John because they had more room for me than Jenny. I would live across the hall, and I could still see her every day. Aunt Eva could take better care of me because Eva was older and had more time for me. The day we were moving, my Uncle John came and got us in his car after the moving men took all our stuff. On the way to our new home, my uncle John got distracted while driving and his car got hit by a bus. I don't really remember much after that," Angelina took a deep breath and paused for a few minutes.

"When I woke up a few days later, I was in a hospital, lying in a bed in a dark room, and there was no one else there with me. I felt all alone. A nurse came in, and I was crying. I didn't know what happened. She checked on me and told me she would call my aunt and tell her I was awake. I was expecting her to call my aunt Jenny, but that was not the case. Father Patrick came in to visit me. He was the one that told me what had happened. He told me about the car accident and that my Aunt Jenny and Uncle John had gone to heaven to be with my mom and dad and grandma. At that moment, I was nine years old, and I was all alone in the world. All my family members were gone."

Angelina paused for another moment; she wiped her tears away, and then kept talking, looking into Dina's eyes.

"I asked Father Patrick why God hated me so much. Why he kept taking everyone away from me to go live in heaven with him, but he didn't want me. Father Patrick held me in his arms and told me that God loved me very much, that God had a special plan for me, and that it wasn't my time to go live in heaven yet.

"After that, my aunt Eva became my legal guardian. So I wouldn't have to go live in foster care. My aunt who was married to my Uncle John raised me as her own child. My aunt and uncle didn't have kids, so it was just the two of us, until she remarried when I was sixteen," Angelina remembered. "She now has children of her own. I still live in her building and see her every day.

I graduated from college for drug and alcohol counseling and social work. Now I am working on my psychology degree. I just love to learn, it is the best thing for me. Between school and church, that's what keeps me sane. I'm twenty-four years old. I have my own apartment, and I work at a community center. I run a youth program, and I also work at women's shelter part-time on weekends.

"I still don't have a lot of friends outside of work and school. Although, I get along with most people and I have friends in class, I have often found it difficult to make a connection with people.

"I guess Harrison is my friend. He lives in my building, and he is my aunt's nephew by blood. He is also a college student and we hang out sometimes. He lost his parents when he was a teenager, so he doesn't bother me about mine. We get along well. Eva is pretty much all he has too, so he does a lot of family things with us.

"So that is pretty much my life story. Do you have any questions?" Angelina asked Dina.

Dina sat for a moment, keeping her professionalism in mind. She maintained her composure, though she herself felt a sense of overwhelm.

"Wow, you are a very impressive young lady. You have been through so much, and yet you still have so much faith in God and in humans. I'm basing that on your career choice and from what you've told me here today," Dr. Hayford paused to take a drink of water and then spoke. "You obviously have a profound inner strength, and this has helped to get to where you are today. You put yourself through school, which couldn't have been easy," Dina Hayford said.

"Well, I have received a lot of scholarships and grants, and my parents had life insurance as well, so that all helped. I have always had my aunt and her husband Henry's help. We get along very well he treats me just like I was his kid," Angelina answered in a soft, sweet voice. "I went to college right away when I was seventeen and had two diplomas in three years. Whenever I feel like I can't handle what I am going through, I turn to God and my parents. I ask for help and guidance, and somehow I get the strength to get through,"

"Wow, I am just so impressed by you and your story. It's amazing. I do have another question. It may be a difficult one but try and answer it honestly. How do you feel about the men who killed your parents?" asked Dr. Hayford.

Angelina took a deep breath, got up, and walked to the window and looked outside for a few minutes. Then walked back and sat down in the big black chair across from Dina.

"I don't really know how to explain how I feel about those men. I really don't think about them much. I know that I hate them for what they did. But I also know that they ruined their own lives because of a bad choice. They were stupid, and because of what they did, I lost my parents, and they went to jail. It's so upsetting because the men had families, and they just threw it all away. They not only ruined my family's life and their own lives, but they ruined the lives of their own families. I feel sorry for their children, even though I hate them so much for what they did," Angelina responded.

Dina just sat there for a minute, looking at the girl sitting in front of her in amazement and hanging on to every word she said. "Angelina, you are amazing. Most people would say, 'I hope those men rot in jail.' But you feel empathy for their children. You see past your own pain and grief. You are right I will always remember you. You should be an inspirational speaker. I teach a class. I know it would be hard, but if you ever decided you want to share your story, I would love to have you come and share with my students. I think your story could help a lot of people. You have overcome so much in your life, and all you want to do is help others. If there were more people like you in this world, it would be a better place. Your parents would be so proud of who you are," said Dina, looking into Angelina's big brown eyes.

Tears were running down Angelina's cheeks, yet she had a

smile on her face. "You think my parents would be proud of me? Boy, I hope so. No one has ever told me before that I am amazing. I think that is the nicest thing anyone has ever said about me. Thank you. Today has been really good for me. I don't know if I am ready to share my story with people yet. I have kept it hidden away for so long. Maybe someday, I will," Angelina said blowing her nose. "So when do I have to come back?"

Dina was looking at her watch, and she noticed that they had gone way over the allotted time. Good thing she didn't have anyone booked right after. She just missed her lunch break today.

"I have everything I need from you. I will pass on my information to the college, and you should be able to start placement after that. Do you already have a placement set up? Because if you don't have one and if you are interested, you could work here for me?" asked Dina.

Angelina had a smile on her face and was calm, cool, and collected. "Thank you. I have applied at a few places, but I am interested to see all that goes on in a therapist's office. Can I let you know later?" asked Angelina, excited and feeling good about herself.

"Yes, of course. Just let me know whenever you can. The position is yours if you want it. I don't often take on students, so just let me know. Well, I have another patient coming in soon, so I will give you my card, and you can call me whenever you like to. Thank you for coming and sharing your story with me." Dina got up from her chair, and so did Angelina. They both walked over to the door and shook hands.

"Thank you for listening. It was very nice to meet you. I'll be in touch," Angelina said as she walked out of Dina's office.

CHAPTER 2

Angelina was on her way home to have dinner with her aunt Eva, Henry, and Harrison, as well as her twin cousins, Lilly and Josh. It was a long bus ride form Dina's office to her apartment building. Her mind was busy with thoughts. She thought about her parents, and she thought about what the therapist suggested—about telling her story and helping people. For as long as Angelina could remember, she loved helping others. It filled her with a sense of purpose. It made her smile and filled her with warmth, and this was why she loved to help others.

She got off the bus, right in front of her apartment building. Aunt Eva was walking with bags of groceries. Angelina approached her, and noticed that she was struggling with the bags a little, Angelina helped her aunt with the groceries as they went into the building.

Eva is forty-five years old, has short blonde hair and blue eyes. She was short in stature, with a small frame. Eva takes care of herself, and always wears nice clothes and jewelry.

"So how did your therapist appointment go today? You look like you have been crying," Eva asked.

"It went well, and yes I cried a lot, but it was good for me to talk about my parents and my family. I told her everything, and she was really nice to me," said Angelina. "She told me that many people have great difficulty coping well with tragedy. She said she was impressed with how far I have come in my life and how I still have so much faith. I told her that I was lucky to still have you in my life. She also spoke with me about a placement and was encouraging. She actually offered me a placement in her office."

Eva was very quiet as they climbed up the stairs of the apartment building. She just listened to Angelina talk, and when they made it to apartment 3, she pulled out the keys from her purse and opened the door, letting Angelina in with the groceries. Angelina walked into the kitchen and put the groceries on the counter.

Eva and Henry had just finished renovating their apartment. They'd spent a considerable amount of time, remodeling. They'd taken out a few walls and took over two apartments, making their apartment very large. The redecorated, creating a look and feel that was more spacious and open-concept.

The kitchen was beautiful and formal, with a bar and stools complimenting elegant black appliances and marble countertops with wooden cabinets. There were hardwood floors throughout, lending to the overall ambiance of the apartment. The living room was painted in a soft brown color and there was a white fireplace and a fifty-two-inch plasma television mounted on the wall. Large comfortable couches in dark green earth tones suited the wooden coffee table and side tables. There were warm family pictures hung upon the walls.

"You talked about your parents and about me and *John?*" Eva spoke in a very soft, sweet voice. A tear rolled down her face, and Angelina gave her aunt a hug.

"We don't have to talk about it if you don't want to," she told her aunt.

"I am OK. Sorry. I just didn't think you would talk about me and John, that's all. It's so hard to think about him. I loved him so much," Eva said shaking her head.

"Well, Eva, you and Uncle John have a part in my life story, and you are all the family I have now. So you are very important in my life." Angelina replied.

Eva hugged her niece in a firm but gentle manner. "I love you," Eva said and then she let her go.

Eva began putting away food, and when she was finished, she began to make dinner.

"So, she offered you a placement with her? That sounds exciting," Eva said.

"Well, I am a psych student, so becoming a therapist could be an option. I don't know yet, I don't have to decide today." Responded Angelina.

Angelina started setting the table for dinner, while her aunt was cooking. Her cousins came home from school, and she decided she would play with them in the living room. Finally Henry and Harrison came home and they all had dinner together.

Henry was Eva's husband. He was a very tall man with a slim build, green eyes, and dirty blond hair. He was a very sweet and loved his family very much. He was a mental health professional and had his own practice. At which he made very good money. Eva worked part-time at an art gallery, and they ran the apartment building. So they were very wealthy.

Dinner was good, although no one said much. Until, The twins sang the song they learned at school. After dinner, Angelina and Harrison washed up and then said good-bye to everyone. As they were both walking up to their apartments, Harrison looked at her differently tonight.

"Angelina, I rented a movie, and I was wondering if you wanted to hang out and watch it with me?" he asked so nervous that he was almost shaking.

Angelina was tired. She had a long and emotionally hard day and didn't really want to. But something about the way he asked—in such a desperate way—made her not want to let him down.

"Yes, I will hang out and watch a movie with you," She said as she was unlocking the door to her apartment. "You go get the movie, and I'll make us popcorn and hot chocolate."

Harrison looked happy. He ran into his apartment without

saying a word, as if he was worried that if he took too long, she might change her mind.

Harrison Plushy was twenty-fives year-old, taking drug and alcohol counseling as his second college course. He already had a diploma in business. Harrison was born in Canada but is of Italian descent. His mom was born in Canada and his dad was born in Italy. He had dark brown hair and big brown eyes with long eyelashes. His skin had a sun-kissed glow to it and he had a baby face with a warm smile. He was physically fit, with a muscular build and stood about six feet tall. Altogether he was an attractive young man, tempered with shyness.

As he came running into her apartment. "I have the movie," Harrison said. He was so excited that she said yes.

"Hey, just pop in the movie, I'm just making the popcorn. I will be there in a minute," Angelina said from the kitchen.

"So what movie did you rent, anyway?" Angelina asked as she brought the popcorn and the hot chocolate and set them down on the coffee table.

"*Love Letters*." Harrison replied. Then he smiled at her, and they both laughed in a playful way.

"You rented *Love Letters*, for real? Why did you do that?" she questioned him as she shook her head and laughed even more.

"I thought you would like to see it," he said, blushing. Feeling a little surprised and embarrassed by the question, Harrison changed the subject. "How was your appointment today?"

Angelina was mad for a second because she knew that her aunt had told him. Then she realized that if she knew about his life and what happened to his parents then he probably knew about hers too.

She thought about how she felt talking about her life today, and it made her feel better. She thought it might be nice to have a friend to talk to sometimes and maybe he was in need of a friend too. Considering they both had no parents and took the same program in school, they definitely had things in common.

"It went well. It was hard—talking about what happened to my family—but afterwards, I felt better," she answered him. "You know what I mean?"

She looked at him. He put his head down and didn't say a word. Angelina put her hand on his back.

"You know it's nice to have a friend to talk to, and I am here if you need me," she said in a sweet comforting voice.

Harrison looked up at her. "How old were you when your parents died?" he asked her nervously.

Angelina felt weird. She had never talked about this stuff with anyone other than Father Patrick. But it felt good to talk to him, and she could sense that he needed to talk, too.

"I was seventeen when my parents died in a plane crash. They went on a second honeymoon, and on the way home, something went wrong, and the plane went down. There were no survivors," Harrison continued to talk, not waiting for a reply to his question.

"It was a horrible tragedy. Sixty-seven people died on that plane. It's been so hard without my parents. I miss them so much. I can't even explain everything I feel."

As his eyes filled with tears, he turned his head away from her and wiped his face with his shirt. He didn't want her to see him cry, but at the same time, he felt so comfortable talking to her.

"I was five. I don't have as many memories of my parents as you would have of yours. But they were killed in a bank robbery. There were twenty people left in the bank that day, but only my parents died. I watched the whole thing as I was hiding in the playhouse. I remember everything about that day right down to what shoes I was wearing. I feel the same way. I can't find the words to explain how I feel, because I feel so many things," Angelina responded. "Broken is what I use to explain how I feel. It's the only word that fits."

Harrison turned back to her. They were both sitting side by side on the couch, and he took her hand and just held it for a while. He looked into her eyes but didn't say a word; it was like he didn't have to.

The two of them were communicating, but not through words. The tragic event they shared seemed to form an unspoken bond between them. Neither of them was paying any attention to the movie.

They shared stories about their lives and things they have experienced. It was amazing for Angelina to feel connected to someone else, as she did with Harrison. She shared a part of her soul with him, and he didn't laugh at her or walk away; he just became more interested. It was funny that they knew each other for a long time but never opened up like that before. They talked all night until they both fell asleep on the couch.

Angelina's apartment was small with two bedrooms and had a little kitchen with a living /dining room combination. Most of her furniture was antique, as it was all handed down to her by her aunt. It actually was all her Uncle John's furniture, and he had a liking for antiques. The walls were of taupe color, and she had a dark wooden table with a matching hutch and dark red couches.

A mahogany coffee table and a big stone fireplace were situated in the living room making a comfortable atmosphere. In the middle of the living room, on the fireplace mantle, was a picture of Angelina and her parents and some candles. One bedroom was like an office space, with shelves from wall-to-wall that were full of books. The other bedroom had old dark wooden furniture, with bluish-gray walls and a sliver bedspread.

When Angelina woke up, she realized she was in Harrison's arms. She didn't move right away; she kind of liked the feeling. Never really having a boyfriend before, she'd never awoken with someone holding on to her. She felt safe and happy.

This was weird. She had always looked at Harrison as a kind of dorky. As she lay there, she stared at him. For the first time, she really saw how beautiful he was. She lay there in his arms, admiring him with his perfectly chiseled face, golden skin, his thick chocolate brown hair and his little ears. She looked at him as if she had never really seen him before. She looked at his prefect full lips and his thick eyebrows. Everything about him was appealing to her now, but he never was before. She realized she had feelings for him.

He opened his eyes, and they both got up and looked to see what time it was.

"It's only eight thirty. Good, I'm not late," Harrison said. "I am sorry for falling asleep on you and I'm sorry but I have to go. I have class at nine," As he got up and she walked him to the door.

"Do you want to have dinner with me tonight? I work till six, but afterwards, we could go out or order in and eat here," Angelina spoke so fast that even she didn't hear what she had said. She felt very nervous and embarrassed. This was Harrison, her dorky friend from across the hall.

But something had changed; she had opened herself up and had seen him in a new way, and now, he was Harrison, the guy she really liked. She put her head down, as she waited for him to respond.

Harrison looked so happy that he had the biggest smile on his face. "Yes, I would love to have dinner with you," he said. After pausing for a minute he asked, "As friends?"

Angelina shut her eyes and kept her head down. She didn't want to look at him, as she felt he thought of her only as a friend. She was surprised about that because she had always thought he had a thing for her. She held her head down with disappointment.

"As friends or as a date?" he asked nervously. "I don't want to be thinking it's a date all day only to find out later that you don't feel that way. So tell me now." He was as nervous as she was and she was feeling very happy.

He put his hand to her chin and lifted her head so that he could see her face. He gazed into her eyes, and he waited for her answer.

"A date." She said softly with smiling eyes.

"Great!" Harrison exclaimed, attempting to hide his sense of joy underneath the guise of a modest posture. He left the apartment, grinning from ear to ear.

Angelina was so happy. She'd never felt this way before. She got dressed and was ready to face her busy day of school and work. She thought about Harrison the entire day and was excited about their date. She had trouble concentrating on almost everything else. When she got home from work, she was nervous and could feel butterflies in her stomach. She didn't know what to wear; but before she could change or even look in the mirror, there was a knock at the door.

She answered the door; it was Harrison. He looked so good. He was wearing a black polo golf shirt with khaki pants and white running shoes. He had black sunglasses on his head, and Angelina was captivated by the smell of his cologne. He normally dressed like a real dork, and now, he had a preppy kind of style going, and Angelina was again pleasantly surprised.

He was holding beautiful, fresh cut white lilies in one hand, and in the other, he was holding a big brown paper bag that said *date night* on it. He had a big smile on his face.

"Hi, I just got home, and I haven't changed yet or showered or anything. And you look so good. What did you do? Go get a makeover or something?" She smiled.

"So you like?" he asked, smiling. "I needed some new clothes, and the girl at the store was very helpful. You can shower, and I will set everything up while you get ready."

He looked at her with a smile on his face.

"OK then. Come in, and I'll be quick," Angelina said. She was curious to see what he had planned.

Angelina hopped into the shower. Harrison got everything out; he put the flowers in a vase on the table, and he set the table, pulling out Chinese food from the *date* bag. He then set candles out everywhere and lit them. He put some candies and chocolates on the coffee table along with three movies.

He dimmed the lights and turned on soft music. Angelina came out, and she was wearing a simple white knit dress. Her long hair was styled curly, with a white headband just holding it off her face. They both just stood there, waiting for the other to talk first.

"Wow! You did all this for me? How sweet!" she said as she

looked around the room she was full of joy and he could see it on her face.

Harrison walked over to her and grabbed her by the hand and touched her face as he looked into her eyes. "You look like an angel. That's what I'm going to call you—my angel," he said in a soft voice, and she smiled and had goose bumps all over her body.

"My mom used to call me Angel. No one has called me that since I was five. Thank you," Angelina replied in appreciation.

They both just stood there, looking at each other. Then Harrison pulled Angelina closer to his body and touched her face. He bent his head down and placed his lips on hers and awaited her response. She moved closer to him and wrapped her arms around him, and the two became locked in a gentle and sweet kiss. It was nice, and it lasted a few minutes. As they broke away and looked at each other, they smiled.

"I just had to do that. I don't think I could have waited until the end of the evening. I have wanted to kiss you since the first day I met you," Harrison said as his face turned red.

"You have known me for five years and you have wanted to kiss me for that long? And you had to wait until I asked you out?" Angelina said giggling.

"OK, well, I am a little shy around you because I have never met anyone like you before, and I mean that in a good way." Harrison could feel an excited nervousness, as he noticed he was beginning to ramble on. He was looking at her with a funny look on his face, feeling a bit like a teenager in high school. Angelina smiled.

"So what's the plan for tonight? I am so hungry," she said as she rubbed her tummy. Harrison, with great relief, smiled at Angelina.

"Chinese food and movies, but I also brought board games, just in case you wanted to do something different." He replied.

They sat down on the couch and put on a movie to watch while they ate. They didn't talk through this one, both of them feeling a little nervous. When the movie was over, they opened a bottle of wine.

"So what games did you bring?" Angelina asked well having a sip of her wine.

"Well, I didn't know what you would be up for, so I brought monopoly, the game of life, twister, and battleship," He said "Do you want to play one?"

"Did you really bring twister?" Angelina said joking with a laugh. "You pervert," Angelina said jokingly, with a laugh.

"No I just—"

Angelina cut him off, "Let's play twister then. It's OK with me, but if you look up my dress, I'll punch you," she said, smiling, with a sweet look on her face as she opened the game box.

They played twister for a while until they both got so twisted into each other that Angelina fell on top of Harrison. Her lips found his, and his hands found her body. It was much more intense than their first kiss was, and it lasted a lot longer. His hands were all over her body, and her hands were all over his. His lips met her neck.

"Is this what you had in mind when you thought about us playing twister?" she asked with nervous laughter.

"Well, I only hoped I would be so lucky," he said, feeling slightly embarrassed at his confession.

They sat up looking at each other, and then cleaned up the game. They decided to put on another movie and lay down on the couch, where they stayed all night in each other's arms.

Every night that week, they hung out, talked, watched movies, and fell asleep in each other's arms, falling more and more for each other. Everything was going great.

One morning, Angelina woke up to Harrison sitting on the floor beside her, watching her sleep. He had a cup of coffee in his hand. He just sat there, looking at her. She stretched and sat up and looked at him.

There were coffee and muffin waiting on the coffee table for her.

"What time is it?" she asked, a little worried that she might have slept to long.

"Don't worry, my angel, it's only seven thirty."

She sighed with relief. "Thank you for breakfast. I have a

busy day today and tomorrow. I have class till two and then I will work till ten at the community center. I'm glad we are at least having breakfast together, because I don't know when I will see you next. Unless you want to come over tonight and watch a movie, but I might just fall asleep on you," she said, smiling. All she really wanted to do was sleep with his big, strong arms holding her, she really felt safe.

"Well, it's up to you. If you're not too tired when you come home and you want to see me, just knock on my door. If you don't come, I'll know you were just too tired, and then maybe, we can go out this weekend on a real date," he responded.

"OK, that sounds good to me," she said. After they were done with their coffees and muffins, Harrison cleaned up and then kissed Angelina on the forehead.

"I have to go to class. I'll see you later," he said. She got up and walked him to the door.

"Harrison, I have never really done this before, so I don't know what this is. Are we together?" she asked, really nervous.

"Yes, Angel, you are my girl," he said as he kissed her cheek and hugged her real tight.

CHAPTER 3

That day was just another ordinary day for Angelina—she went to class and talked to the same people she talked to every day. She had the same lunch (veggie pizza) she had every Thursday in the cafeteria, and then she worked out for a half hour at the school gym before her next class. After class, she took the same bus to work, worked with all the same kids and staff as she always did. Other than Angelina being euphorically happy, that day was just like any other day.

Angelina worked with teens at the community center. The center was not in a very nice part of the city, and there were a lot of gangs in the area. Some of the kids in her program were former gang members. So sometimes, there was gang-related trouble, like vandalism. The cops have been had to be called to come break up the fights.

Angelina was working with Adam and Jeff, other counselors at the center. They had a big basketball game going on in the gym with the kids. When a big group of unhappy looking teens walked in, they were not there to sign up to be in the program.

There were about nine of them—all teen boys. They were of mixed races— white, Latin, Black. They couldn't be much older than fourteen, and they looked angry.

Angelina grouped all the kids together. She could see that Adam had his cell phone in his pocket, and she told him to be ready to all the cops, in case any trouble unfolded.

Every one of the kids could sense that something was going on, and they rushed for cover behind their staff.

"If you're here to hang out and play a game and cause no trouble, then you are welcome to stay. But if not, then please leave," Angelina said, looking at the gang of boys.

The boys walked to the middle of the gym. All were wearing white t-shirts, dark blue jeans, and a green bandana around their heads. One boy, who looked to be the oldest, stepped forward and gave her a nasty look, and his body language told her that things were going to get ugly.

"Listen, bitch, we're not going anywhere because we are sick of you, stupid rich white girl, stealing our family. Jamal, Marquis, and Lang belong to us," the boy said, and he spit on the ground. "They are part of our family, and no one just leaves their family. It doesn't work that way unless they're dead."

Angelina looked over at Adam, who had already notified the police department quietly, via text message. She could tell from his reaction that the police were on their way.

The oldest boy, who appeared to be in charge, spoke again.

"Just let my boys leave, and there won't be any problems," he said as he glared at her.

Raising his shirt, he revealed a Glock 45 he had tucked into his jeans. Instinctively, Angelina moved to the side, blocking the children from the view of the gang. She quickly and subtly, put her hand behind her back, quietly snapping her fingers at Jeff and Adam, who were with the group of children. Jeff looked at Angelina's hand as her fingers quietly snapped.

Angelina gently motioned with her hand, behind her back, moving all the kids as close to the door, without letting the gang notice. She glanced over to the three boys that once belonged to that gang. All were under the age of fourteen. They looked so terrified, and they didn't want to leave.

"When I distract them, sneak the kids out as fast as you can. No matter what, get the kids out," Angelina whispered to Jeff with a scared look on her face.

Angelina started walking closer to the gang, "I really don't want any problems, but I can't let the boys leave with you. They don't want to go. Is there something else I could do to help you boys today?" Angelina asked, hoping to appeal to some sense of compassion, all the while remaining as calm as she could.

The oldest boy that appeared to be in charge was mad; she could see it in his flushed face. He pulled out the gun, cocked it, and pointed it right at her. "Listen, bitch, those boys are going to either leave with me or leave in body bags. What way do you want to see this play out?"

Angelina looked behind her to see if any of the kids had gotten out of the gym. She noticed most of the kids had gotten out, so she knew they would be safe. She realized Marquis and Lang had made it out, but Jamal was still in there, hiding and shaking. When she turned her head back to face the boy with the gun in his hand, she knew he had figured out that the others were gone. He raised the gun and pointed it at Jamal, who was only thirteen years old.

Angelina ran as fast she could to get in front of the young boy to protect him. She didn't think about what was going to happen. She didn't care about herself. All she knew was she had to save the kids; nothing else mattered to her at that moment. She shielded Jamal, and the last thing she heard was a bang. And before she knew what had happened, the cops were there, and she was lying on the ground with a bullet in her stomach.

The pain was so severe that she was trembling. She felt someone holding her hand; she looked over, and it was Jamal. He was alive! Thank God, he was OK. For half a second, she thought his face was the most beautiful thing she had ever seen at that moment. All she thought about was that he was still alive, and for that one moment she didn't feel the pain. She looked all around, making sure all the kids had gotten out safely. Her vision was going blurry, and she couldn't breathe, she gasped for air. The pain was burning, and then she just saw darkness. Then paramedics came, and they worked on her. They got her on the stretcher, and got her in the ambulance and worked on her, but it was too late her heart had stopped beating.

CHAPTER 4

All of a sudden, the darkness turned into light, the brightest light she'd ever seen, and there was music, the most amazing music. It was like a symphony with beautiful harmonies, like the songs of birds. The cold faded, and she felt warm. She felt the loveliest feelings of warmth and comfort and safety. Wonderful feelings that no words could ever do justice came over her and held her body, and then Angelina opened her eyes completely.

The most beautiful lights came into her sight, and it was accompanied by the most beautiful music. Everything was amazing. She tried to make out where she was and what she was seeing, but it wasn't possible. She looked down at her feet, and it looked like she was standing on a cloud. When she looked up, it was like she was looking at the sun, but it was more beautiful than she had ever seen it before. No words could describe how lovely it was. It was so hot, but the heat was perfect.

Everything was perfect, even though she could not fully comprehend where she was. She saw things so clearly, the flowers in all different colors, reds and blues and yellows and pinks and purples more vibrant and luxurious than she had ever seen before. The trees were astonishing she got lost for a moment just looking at their breath taking beauty. She saw a babbling brook and a river that ran into the clouds. The water of the river appeared to be shimmering. It looked like the most beautiful meadow, but on top of clouds. She was not scared and wasn't worried about the kids at the center, and it was as though all her pain and worry were many miles away from her. She wasn't thinking about what had just happened to her. She didn't even think about her aunt Eva or even about Harrison. She found herself within this moment, just trying to take in all the beauty of this place.

Where could she be? She looked around, not wanting to miss one moment or one thing of this lovely place. She wasn't alone; she saw a woman, the most beautiful angelic woman. She had long dark brown hair, and it did glowed like it was made from gold. She was wearing a white lace dress with and she had a shimmering glow to her. Her face had the most perfect smile—so very warm and gentle. Angelina again heard a song, it was even more beautiful. She recognized the music as she had heard it before.

Then when she looked at the woman, tears began falling down her face. She knew this woman; she was overwhelmed with excitement and love. It had been all she had wanted for so long. The beautiful Angel standing in front of her was her mother. She came closer to her. They stood there, looking into each other's eyes for a long time. It was a perfect moment. She hugged her mother so tightly and for so long, she did not want to let go. For a brief moment, she was scared that if she let go, then her mother would be gone forever. She closed her eyes as she felt her mother's arms around her. She felt years of love all in one moment and she was over whelmed and over joyed.

When she opened her eyes, she saw the most amazing man. He seemed to be gliding or floating toward her and her mother, and she knew it was her father. He was glowing. She had never seen him look so beautiful, even though he looked just like she remembered. He was tall and thin and had dark hair and green eyes. He was very handsome but even more so now that he was an Angel. She looked at his perfect face and she saw all her accomplishments in his eyes all the moments he wasn't there for. All those times she wished she could have shared them with her father. He saw every minute of her life and he was there with her every step of the way. She felt how proud he was of her and she felt more loved in that moment than she had ever felt in her whole life. She took comfort in knowing that he never missed a moment.

They all hugged each other for so long and they didn't speak. In this place, there was no need to speak. They could feel what each other were feeling and thinking. It was the most beautifully amazing family reunion. Father Patrick had told her that one day she would be with her parents again, and it had come true. Everything was perfect and there were no words to describe how incredible that moment with her family was.

They all started moving; it was if they were floating on the clouds and passing through the meadow. She saw other people there, some she recognized some she didn't. Everyone is in white and that's when she realized she was in a lovely white dress herself and she felt beautiful. She saw her Aunt Jenny who looked like a goddess, her hair was flowing and her eyes sparkling, she sent Angelina a kiss that warmed her heart. She saw her Uncle John and he smiled at her as he touched her hand. She could feel how much he loved her and how happy he was to see her again as she floated on bye with her parents.

I must be in heaven nothing could be more beautiful or more perfect than this. Everyone looked at her as they heard her thoughts and pointed to the right.

She saw a river with the most beautiful crystal clear blue water. She was captivated by such a sight; such beautiful things existed indeed. Another magnificent sight was a big ship boarding people. The ship looked like it was made out of gold and sparkled with great glory. The river ran to a huge white castle. It was shimmering and radiant. Angelina thought she was to board the ship, but she kept floating, passing it by. For a moment, she wanted to go up to the castle.

All the people in white were still pointing to the right like they were frozen just there to guide her in the right direction. Angelina kept floating by, weightlessly and effortlessly. She felt as if her heart was carrying her along.

She came to a winding staircase with big white railings. Each step looked like it was made out of the most radiant marble. However, the people didn't walk up the stairs, the stairs moved; it was so incredible. At top of the stairs, there was the most illuminating light, the most perfect sight ever. Angelina was hoping that she would get to go there to see that light—but she just kept floating on by.

She saw many people going up the stairs. It looked like they were receiving wings. Angelina wanted to go up there so badly. She wanted to receive the light and get her wings more than she ever wanted anything, but she just kept floating by.

Then on the right, she saw the biggest shimmering gates, more beautiful than humanly possible, glowing in all their purity. She could see inside of them, and it was like a glowing city of love. She could feel so much love as she stood there taking it all in. She was so excited as joy filled her heart. She thought *this must be where she was going, where I belonged.*

However, she kept floating. There was a man in a white suit. There was something about him—he was different than the others. He appeared older than them and he was very serious.

Angelina did not know this man. He had a very serious expression on his face but had wisdom and great radiance of love in his eyes. Behind him were a set of wings.

The wings were different than one might expect wings to be—no feathers, and they weren't really white, seemingly of the purest light; they were almost transparent.

They were astonishing, and it was as if they were glowing and so was he. He just stood there looking at her. She didn't know what to do or say. Up to this moment, everything just happened, and she was taking in every second. The man spoke in a very deep, clear voice that carried like an echo.

"Angelina, it is not your time, and that is why you have not entered into heaven." The man put his hand to his face, like he was thinking.

"If heaven is all one place, then why are there different entrances to get there?" she asked curiously, looking at the Angel standing in front of her.

The man looked at her with a smile on his face. "Because everyone sees and feels things differently. Heaven is perfect so it is everything one would want it to be," he said in a comforting voice. He looked at her like he was so happy to see her. "Angelina, you are a very special girl, and you have a special purpose on earth as you will in heaven. There is still so much left for you to do, so many lives you've yet to touch. You are what we call a spirit guild or a living Angel."

Angelina felt confused. *How am I an Angel? Almost every person I have ever loved died around her.* She kept listening to the man talk.

"You help people find their way just by being you. You touch people's hearts every day. You saved your aunt Eva, when she took you in and took care of you. She found a new sense of hope, and her heart once again opened up. Having you in her life has helped to strengthen her spirit, and she in turn has strengthened yours. You go to church and reach out to others, and you have so much faith in God that your light shines and touches everyone around you."

He spoke with so much passion. She listened to every word like it lingered in the air.

"Without you, your aunt would have stopped going to church, and she would have never been open to new possibilities. She would have never met Henry and fell in love with him and had the kids she always wanted. Without you, she would have been all alone and as you would have been if you didn't have her. Its the small things you do that, you don't even know you do.

You helped Dr. Hayford—after listening to your story, she began to reevaluate her life, and she has forgiven her husband for the hurt full things he has done and now they are working on their marriage. They have begun communicating again and remembering why they fell in love in the first place. You are special. Your purpose is not to invent something amazing or cure a disease but to shine as who you are. The lightest touch can have a profound influence. Angelina, you do and care so much for others. You have seldom put aside time for yourself. You've helped Harrison more than anyone could ever know."

Hearing his name sent shivers down her spin and goose bumps all over her body. It was like his name echoed in her ear, "Harrison, Harrison, Harrison . . ."

"A few years ago, he was going through a hard time. He was failing out of business school and he was blaming God for taking his parents away. He didn't want to live anymore. He wanted to end his life. Then you befriended him, invited him to go to church with you, and talked to him about your faith. You helped him study. He needed you, and you were there every time. Even when you sometimes felt overwhelmed by matters in your own life, you were still always there for him. When one gives selflessly and willingly, one also receives. You helped him. You have always been an Angel, Angel, Angel." The word echoed in her mind. "He knows how special you are. Although you can't see it, he does."

Angelina didn't understand why he was telling her about all this—making her think about the people she loved and making her think about Harrison. Angelina had tears in her eyes. She didn't even know if they were happy or sad. She looked behind her and saw her family, the family that she had waited so long to be with again, and she was still for a moment. She wanted to stay there with them forever. But a small part of her still felt like she was not supposed to go to heaven just yet. That's when she knew that she couldn't die or she wouldn't still have such a strong attachment to earth and her life. She looked at the man with a smile on her face.

"Please, just send me wherever I need to be."

CHAPTER 5

There were three paramedics—one driving and two in the back with Angelina's body. Anderson was the one working on her when she died; he hadn't given up on her, not yet. Tom was the other paramedic. He had become discouraged after trying to revive her for several minutes.

"She's gone, man, let her go," Tom said to Anderson, patting him on the back.

Anderson had tears running down his face as he continued to work on her. No matter how many calls they get when a life hangs in the balance, it never gets easier.

The hospital was twenty-five minutes away, but he wasn't going to give up until he had to. Even though Angelina had stopped breathing there was still a chance she could live. After thirty minutes with no oxygen to the brain, she probably wouldn't wake up, and if she did, she might very well have some handicap or brain damage. Anderson felt something, something that drove him to keep trying, guidance perhaps—a subtle nudge or whisper in his ear. He didn't want to let her go.

When they got to the hospital, he had to stop working on her. He put his hand on her chest and prayed, "God, please, don't let this one die. She just saved the lives of a whole bunch of kids. I don't know this girl, but I believe the world still needs her." Tears ran down his face.

When they took her body into the hospital, Angelina was pronounced DOA. They gave the nurse her information so she could contact the family to identify the body and say their good-byes. They took her lifeless body to a room and laid her on a bed until the family would arrive. Anderson grabbed her by the wrist to pay his respect to the girl he couldn't save, and he was startled when Angelina body started shaking.

He screamed and called for the nurse to come. "She is not dead!" he exclaimed. "She's seizuring," He was panicking. He knew in his heart that this one was special.

The nurse paged the on call doctor, and they worked to stabilize her, before taking her into surgery. They worked quickly and diligently, as every second counted.

When Eva arrived at the hospital, Angelina was still in surgery, having the bullet removed, so she sat in the waiting room, crying and praying that her niece would live.

While she was waiting for some information from someone, her husband Henry showed up with Harrison, who looked like he had been crying for days. He walked into the waiting room and gave Eva a hug and sat down beside her. They all just sat there. No one spoke for a while; all three of them were in shock.

"I am in love with her," he stated abruptly. "I'm in love with her, and she may never get to know that. My heart is breaking, but I keep telling myself that she is going to be OK."

Eva was sitting between Harrison and her husband, Henry; both of them were holding her hands so tightly. She couldn't feel her fingers, and tears just kept falling down on her cheeks.

"I have been here for four hours, and they haven't told me anything yet. All I know that is she is in surgery." said Eva.

Henry went to get them all some coffee, and when he came back, he had a kind of smile on his face. Harrison and Eva wondered as to *why he was smiling*. A moment later, he walked over to them. "You both have to see this, come with me outside for one minute," Henry said.

All three of them walked toward the front doors of the hospital and saw police and press. There were cameras. Hundreds of people were standing outside with candles, praying for the recovery of the girl, who had put aside her own life to save the kids at the community center.

At that moment, Harrison smiled. He felt a sense of peace come over him. "I know now she is going to be all right with all these people praying. God has to listen to all of our prayers. I just know she will be all right."

After Harrison finished speaking, he looked at Henry, who

was talking to Eva. "Eva, they would like a statement from the family. Do you think you could do that?"

Tears were falling down her face, and she couldn't stop them. She was so moved by what she was witnessing; all of these people were here for her niece. She was so surprised by the people that gathered that night in Toronto, who took the time to pray for someone else. She was so unbelievably touched.

"Yes I will speak," she said in a soft voice.

There were lots of reporters asking questions. As cameras were fixated on Eva, she spoke: "Please be quiet, I would like to make a statement. I am not going to be answering any questions right now. I don't know much, aside from being told that my niece is in surgery. I would like to express our deepest thanks to all of you. We are so touched to see so many gathered here. All your prayers and your kindness offers us great hope. Thanks to all the people that are praying for my niece. She is an amazing girl, and I am not surprised at all that she would jump in front of a bullet to save a child. That is just who she is. Today no one else got hurt, because of what my Angelina did. I know that my Angel would take comfort in knowing that she protected the others. Please keep praying. I know she will feel all this love. Our family church is St. Mary's. Please feel free to go there and talk to Father Patrick, who is a good friend of the family. He will know more information as soon as we do. Thank you for all your support."

Eva turned away and walked back into the hospital, and Harrison and Henry followed her. They returned to the waiting room and waited. Finally, after seven hours of waiting, Dr. Kelly came out to speak to the family.

The doctor was a little bald man with glasses. He spoke in a voice that was slightly higher in pitch than one might expect, but his demeanor was kind and gentle. Eva, Henry and Harrison all stood up. Following the doctor down the hallway, they stopped in front of a room.

"Angelina was shot in the stomach, but by some miracle, none of her vital organs were seriously damaged. And we managed to get the bullet out in one piece. Right now she is stable." The doctor said.

Eva had a sense of relief for about half a minute; then the doctor spoke, "What the real concern now is, on the way to the hospital, Angelina stopped breathing, and she didn't have a pulse."

Eva felt her heart skip a beat, and suddenly, she felt a lump in her throat. "Wha what, what are you talking about?" Her voice was shaky as she asked.

"It was really quite miraculous. When Angelina was brought in, she had no vital signs, and then, one of the EMT reported a faint pulse, shortly after she had arrived. Such instances have been reported but are very rare."

"How long was she dead before they revived her?" Eva had a very worried look on her face, and a few tears gathered in her eyes, choking out the question.

"She had no vital signs for about forty-five minutes, and without oxygen to the brain for that long, she may have suffered some brain damage. Unfortunately, she is in a coma, and it is difficult to assess the extent of brain damage. She is in this room, and you can go and see her now. We will keep you posted if her condition changes in any way. All we can do now is wait and see if she wakes up," the doctor spoke clearly but calmly.

The words *if she wakes up* . . . lingered in the air.

Harrison waited in the hallway, while Eva and Henry went into the room to see Angelina. Angelina looked like she was peacefully sleeping, and the expression on her face was like she was having the most incredible dream. Eva sat down on a chair next to the hospital bed and held her hand. She shut her eyes and prayed, "John, if you can hear me, you send her back to me, please help her. Don't let her die this way. This world still needs her. I still need her." Eva cried so much that she could barely get the words out.

"Angel, I love you. I hope you can hear me. I want you to know that you have made my life better, and I will always think of you as my daughter. You are such an amazing person, and I don't think I have told you that enough. I am so proud of you and everything you have accomplished in your life. I am proud of what you did to save those kids today. I know you will do good things in your life, so much more than you already have done. All the families and people that you have helped from the shelter and from the community center, they are all here, praying for you, sweetheart. I hope one day you get to have fun, travel, and experience good things. You have seen so much sadness in your life, and I hope you get to fall in love, and I hope it will be amazing."

Eva stood up and looked at Angelina. Then Henry, who was standing in the room the whole time, walked over, stood behind his wife, and hugged her.

"Angelina, we love you, and we will be here for you always," Henry said as he touched her and let out a few tears, trying to stay strong for his wife.

Both Eva and Henry walked out of the room into the hallway, where Harrison was sitting on the floor with his head down. He looked at both of them, holding back his tears he got up. "Why don't you both go home and get some rest and figure out whatever you need to do? The kids will be waking up soon, and you'll have to get them off to school. I'll stay with her tonight, and I'll call you if she wakes up," Harrison said, hugging Eva.

"Thank you. I'll be back in the morning," Eva said, blowing her noise on a Kleenex.

"Is there anything we can get you before we leave, a coffee or a sandwich?" Henry asked. It was his way of trying to help, he did it out of the kindness of his heart.

"No, I'm fine. I don't need anything. You two just go home and get some rest. It's been a long day, and the next little while is not going to be any easier."

Eva gave Harrison another hug, and she started crying again.

Henry had to pull her away. Henry and Eva left the hospital and went home to take care of their children.

Harrison walked into the hospital room where his Angel lay, hooked up to machines. He felt so helpless just watching and knowing there was nothing he could do to help her. He sat down beside her in a chair and held her hand.

"You can't just kiss me one night and die the next day. That is not fair. You better wake up. I need you in my life," he said as he touched her hand.

He stayed in that chair. He didn't leave her side the whole night. For the next few days, Eva, Henry, Father Patrick, and Harrison sat by her side. They all took shifts so she was never alone. People sent cards and flowers and teddy bears.

CHAPTER 6

It had been three weeks, and Angelina didn't wake up. Though the doctors were very concerned, Harrison was not ready to give up. He talked to her every day. He brought her stuff from her apartment. He played music for her. He even sang to her, not very well, but he did. One night, he climbed into the hospital bed with her and just held her in his arms, and tears fell down his face.

"I am so in love with you. I have been in love with you for years but was too afraid to tell you. You have to wake up. I need you in my life. You make life better. I want to be the best I can be so you will be proud of me. The best time of my life was the last few days when you finally opened up to me. Things were going so perfect, and then you had to go and get shot. What were you thinking?" He touched her face, and tears poured down his cheeks. Then he let out a little laugh.

"Dear God and all the Angels in heaven, please send her back to earth even if she is not meant to be with me. I will even take her place. She needs to live. There are still so many lives she has not touched. I have never wanted anything in my life more than I want her to wake up. Please mom and Dad if you can help her," he prayed and cried and held her close to him until he fell asleep.

It felt like she was floating back into her body. Angelina was waking up. She knew she was alive. She could hear a heartbeat and the noises of the machines that were hooked up to her body. She could smell something, but she didn't know what it was. Her whole body was hurting she could feel the pain. Her eyes were very heavy. They didn't want to open. She felt safe and then she realized that someone was holding her. She remembered that feeling; she knew who it was holding her. She felt safe and comforted. Then just wanting to see his face, she opened her eyes and just looked at him. He looked so beautiful sleeping beside her. She was so happy to see him. She took a deep breath and then looked around the room. Her room was filled with flowers. They were everywhere. She was very confused. She didn't have a lot of friends, so who was all this stuff from? She looked at Harrison. Although it was difficult to move, she touched his face with her hand.

His eyes opened wide. He was so shocked that he burst into tears, and so did she. And then, he touched her face, and they just lay there, looking into each other's eyes.

"Oh, my Angel, you are awake. I am so happy!" he said. "How are you feeling?"

He was so excited that he took a deep breath, trying to calm himself down.

Angelina tried to talk, but it was too hard. She made a sad face and looked at him with tears in her eyes as she touched her throat. He got out of the bed.

"I'm just going to get the nurse. I'll be right back," he said anxiously.

The nurse came in and checked on her and made sure she was stable. "A doctor will come and see you soon. Would you like some water or ice chips to suck on? Your throat must be really dry," the nurse asked in a sweet voice.

She shook her head yes. While the nurse was checking on her, Harrison called Eva to tell her Angelina was awake. The nurse brought her some ice chips to suck on and a cup of water. Harrison sat on the chair beside her bed. Angelina patted the bed, telling him she wanted him to lay down with her.

He got into the bed with her and just held her for a while, without saying a word. Angelina drank some water, and after a little while, she tried talking. She looked at him and in a very slow raspy voice, "I woke up because I could feel your heartbeat." She said.

He smiled with tears in his eyes. "I was hoping if you could feel me, you would wake up. Do you know what happened to you?" he asked her, and her eyes got sad, and she made a pouting face like a sad child.

"I died. I know. I saw my mom and dad." She started crying thinking back to the perfectness of where she was. "It was so beautiful there. Everything was perfect, but I couldn't stay there.

I still have so much to do here on earth," she spoke with so much passion that her voice cracked. She had so much to tell him, but she couldn't, because her body was too tired, and her throat hurt so much.

He just held her in his arms. He didn't want to tell her too much, because he didn't want to upset her. He figured Eva or the doctors would tell her what had happened.

"Are all the kids OK? Did anyone else get hurt?" she asked worriedly in a whisper (as she didn't have much of a voice), getting all excited.

"All the kids are fine. No one else was hurt," he told her.

When Eva walked into the room, Harrison got out of the bed. "I am going to go home and shower. I'll let you visit with Aunt Eva, and I'll come back later." He bent over and kissed her on the forehead.

Eva was confused by that, but she was so happy to see Angelina. She walked over with tears in her eyes and hugged her. Angelina was emotional too.

"How are you feeling, honey?" Eva asked, concerned.

"I am OK. My throat hurts. It's a little hard to talk a lot, my whole body is really stiff, and I have pain in my stomach," she said. As she moved to sit up, she grabbed her stomach and had a painful look on her face.

"Do you remember what happened to you?" Eva asked.

Angelina made a funny face. "Well, I know I died, but I don't know how I died. I remember the kids at the center. I had to make sure they were safe. I remember a bad group of teens bugging us. I remember lying on the ground and in pain, lots of pain," she said, taking a sip of her water.

"Then everything was so beautiful. I have never seen or heard or smelt a more perfect place. My parents were there, and Aunt Jenny, and I saw Uncle John. He smiled at me. I felt so much love there. It was so incredible, but I had to come back. I have to live. There is still so much for me to do in life," Angelina spoke with so much passion that her eyes lit up with hope, but her voice gave out because she was pushing herself too hard. She was just so excited that she wanted to tell her aunt everything.

As Eva was listening to her story, tears kept falling down her face. She believed every word Angelina said. Then a doctor came in to check on Angelina. Eva waited in the hallway and then came back in when he was done.

"Angelina, you seem to be doing amazingly well, but we have to run some test to make sure your brain is healthy," the doctor spoke like he was concerned. "The nurse will be here soon to get you prepped, and I'll see you later,"

When Eva looked at Angelina, she looked so sad and had tears in her eyes. "I got shot!" She sounded like a kid that had lost her favorite toy. She was heartbroken. It was like as if someone had stolen her innocence away. She was breathing really heavy. Eva put her hand on Angelina's shoulder.

"Yes, honey, I am sorry, you did get shot, but you saved the lives of the children at the center. Honey, look at this room. All this stuff was sent here for you from all the families of the kids you saved. People lined up outside of this hospital and prayed for you. You are a hero," Eva said, hugging her.

Angelina was feeling so many things, but she couldn't talk anymore. She needed to rest and she fell asleep.

When Angelina woke up, there were three women and three boys in her room. She didn't know what was going on. Then she recognized the boys from the center. It was Marquis, Lang, and Jamal. Jamal was holding her hand and crying.

"Hey, you don't cry. We are both still alive, and I couldn't be happier that you are here with me right now," she said, holding his hand tightly.

"Angelina, we are all so grateful for what you did for our children. We could never thank you enough," Jamal's mom said. She spoke with so much gratitude in her voice.

"I am just so happy you three are all safe. I am fine, even getting shot can't keep me down for too long. I'll be back at the center soon enough, kicking all your butts at basketball," she said, smiling and looking up at the boys.

"I feel like I need to do something special to repay you for saving me," Jamal said.

"You want to repay me for what I did? OK. Then this is what I want you to do—I want you to always listen to your mother. I want you to go to high school and graduate and then to college. Can you do that for me?"

"Yes, I can do that for you and for me," Jamal said. "That doesn't feel like it's enough though."

"OK. Then I want you to come to my church, every Sunday. I'll be there as soon as I can, so I'll know if you don't show," she said, smiling at him.

"We all will do that, we will all stay in school and go to church," Marquis said, smiling.

The boy's moms were all emotional, and everyone was so happy that she was alive. They all thanked her for what she did to save their children. A big blonde nurse came in and kicked everyone out.

"Hello friends, I am sorry but Angelina needs her rest and I have to change her IV," said the nurse.

After they left, the nurse checked Angelina and made sure she was stable. She then cleaned her up and checked to ensure all the machines were working.

"Well I am all done and there is a really cute young man hanging out in the waiting room and he is dying to see you. He has been here every day for the last few weeks. He sang to you, brushed your hair, and read to you. That boy loves you, girl," the nurse said, smiling. "Can I send him?"

Angelina smiled. She felt joy of just the thought of seeing

him. She was so happy. "Please send him in," she said with a big smile on her face.

"The doctor will be in soon to talk to you about the results of your CAT scan," the nurse said as she was leaving the room.

Harrison walked into the room, looking amazing with his incredible smile on his face. Angelina's face lit up as soon as she saw him. She was overjoyed that he was there for her.

"How are you feeling today?" Harrison asked.

"I am feeling alright. I would love to get out of this bed soon, though," she said. "My whole body hurts."

He climbed into bed with her and wrapped his arms around her and kissed her cheek.

"May be we can talk to the doctor, and maybe I can push you around the hospital in a wheelchair," he said, holding her.

"Yeah, that would be nice. I need to get out of this bed." Replied Angelina

As they were cuddling in her hospital bed, Eva walked in with her family. They were coming for a visit. "OK, what is going on between the two of you? Are you together or something?" Eva asked in a loud voice. She felt like she was being left out.

Harrison opened his mouth to speak, but before he could get a word out, Angelina spoke. "Yes," she said like it was no big deal. "Hello, Lilly and Josh," she said. She was very excited to see her cousins. "Are you to going to come and give me a hug or what?" Angelina said to the kids. Both of them ran over to her and sat on the bed.

"I knew you would be OK!" Lilly said in a happy voice but with sad eyes.

"I missed you, are you ever coming home?" Josh also asked in a sad voice.

Angelina hugged both the kids. "I missed you both, too. I hope I can go home soon, but it's not up to me, it's up to the big doctor. He is the boss," she said, and they all giggled together.

Everyone could tell that Eva was not happy. She was staring at Angelina with her arms folded.

"Let's take the kids to the cafeteria and let the ladies talk," Henry said, looking at Harrison with a let's-get-out-of-here look on his face.

"Bye, Angie," said Josh and Lilly, running out of the room.

Eva sat down in the chair beside Angelina's bed and looked at her with a concerned look on her face.

"So when did things start with you and Harrison, and how come you didn't tell me about this?" Eva said. She wasn't mad, she just felt left out.

Angelina smiled. "It just happened the night we all had dinner together at your place. That night, we hung out afterwards and talked all night. We opened up to each other and talked about our parents. Then the next night, we had Chinese food and watched a movie. We've only kissed. It just happened. That week, we hung out, and then, well, all of this happened. So that's pretty much the story, but I am really happy when he is around, and I think about him all the time." Angelina was glowing as she talked about him. Eva could see how she was falling in love.

"Well, I am so happy for you both. I think you will make a great couple, and he told me that he loves you. I knew for a while that he had a thing for you, but I didn't know you were into him, too," Eva said. Then they both laughed like school girls. It was a special moment for both of them.

A doctor walked into the room to give them the results of the test. Eva was more nervous than Angelina was.

"Well, Ms. Heart, you must have one hell of a guardian Angel, because you are a very lucky girl," the doctor said, smiling.

"Yeah, I have a few Angels actually," she said out loud with a big smile on her face thinking about her family.

"After everything you have been through, it's amazing that you are up moving around and talking. And your tests came back all fine. The CAT scan was clean, and you have no internal bleeding. Your wounds are healing well. We want to keep you here for another few weeks or so to monitor you, and then you will be able to go home. But you probably should take some time off from school and work and just relax and take care of yourself. First, you should not be alone. Make sure you have someone that can help you all the time," the doctor said.

Henry, Harrison, and the kids came back, and they all were

there for a while together, laughing and talking. They all had a good time. They all left, but Harrison stayed with Angelina; he really didn't like leaving her alone at the hospital. A part of him was afraid that if he left she might fall asleep and not wake up again.

"I'll be right back. I have a surprise for you," he said with enthusiasm.

He came back into her room a few minutes later with a wheelchair that had pink balloons tied to it. "Your chariot awaits my dear. I talked to the nurse, and she said it was fine to take you out for a little walk around the hospital," he said with a smile on his face as he held out his hand to help her into the wheelchair.

"Thank you. This is so sweet of you to do this for me. I am so excited. We're going on an adventure," she said in a sweet happy voice.

They went for a tour of the hospital. They came to the elevators, and he pushed her inside and pushed the button to the twentieth floor.

"Where are we going?" she asked, very curious.

"I have a place I want to show you," he said as they were getting off the elevator. He pushed her down the hall. They came to a room that said *Library* on the door, and her face lit up with joy.

"I found the library earlier, and I thought you might want to pick out a book. I know how much you like to read."

"I am so excited. I do have a lot of time on my hands. Having a new book to read would be great."

They went into the library. It wasn't very big, but she was just so happy to be out of her hospital bed and to be with him. She looked through the books and picked out one she wanted to borrow. They hung out in the library for a while. He read a few children's books to her; she laughed. They left the library and walked all over the hospital, talking.

"Are you hungry?" Harrison asked.

"Yes, I could eat." Angelina replied.

They went to the cafeteria. There was dead silence in there. They almost had the whole food court to themselves. They sat there in the dark room and ate dinner together and spent hours just talking.

CHAPTER 7

Harrison opened Angelina's apartment door for her and helped her on to the couch. Eva and Henry brought her bags in and unpacked her stuff for her.

"The community center has granted you a leave of absence for as long as you need, you will always have a job there if you want it," Eva told Angelina.

"The shelter pretty much said the same thing— to take some time off and to heal. Everyone loves you and is thinking about you. The school was very understanding, and based on your grades, you will still be able to graduate. But you will have to work something out for your placement, because all the placements are filled, and you have missed over a month, a normal placement won't work. But once you feel better, they have a few options you can chose from," Eva said. Angelina was feeling overwhelmed, but Eva didn't stop with the information.

"All your bills have been paid for the month. I bought you some food. It's in the fridge. I'll do your laundry, and if there is anything you need help with, you let me know. A nurse will come two times a day to help you bathe and clean and change your dressings. I'm home in the mornings, and I'll come and visit you before I go to work. Henry will bring you anything you need, and Harrison will help you in the evenings. Between all of us, you are in good hands." Eva smiled. She realized she was talking a lot and Angelina looked exhausted.

"Henry and I are going to go and let you rest, but if you think you are up for it, later you can come up for dinner. Or I'll bring some food down to you. If you need me, just call," Eva said as she handed her the cordless phone.

"I want you resting, young lady. Don't worry about anything. This couch is where you need to stay." She bent down and hugged Angelina.

Angelina looked up at Eva, she could tell she was just excited, because she was happy that Angelina was all right.

"Thank you for taking such good care of me, but I am fine. I just need a blanket and a pillow, and I'll be good." replied Angelina.

Henry brought her a blanket and a pillow. "We love you, kiddo," He said, patting her on the head. Even though it was annoying, she knew he did that because he, too, was happy that she was home.

Eva and Henry left. Harrison was sitting on a chair, just looking at her, and she looked at him. She was happy to be home and that he was there with her.

"Is there anything you need or want to do? Is there anything I can get for you?" he asked.

"Well, there is something I would love to do," she said with a funny look on her face. "I'll need your help, but you will probably say no."

"Well, what is it that you would love to do?" he asked with a really curious look on his face.

"I really want to brush my teeth and wash my face, and maybe, you could even wash my hair for me. I know I'm asking a lot, but I feel so gross," she said, making a funny face. "If you help me, I promise to relax for the rest of the night." She smiled at him, with a sweet but sexy look in her eyes.

He looked at her with a smile. "Of course, I will help you," he said like it was no big deal.

He stood up and put his hands out to help her up off the couch. He helped her to the bathroom. She couldn't move her body too much because her stomach was still very sore and she had to be careful not to open her stitches.

He held her head over the bathroom sink, and he poured water over her head. He gently massaged shampoo into her hair. His hand felt amazing. He was so careful not to get soap in her eyes. He rinsed the shampoo from her hair, and he carefully wrapped her head with a towel. He then took a facecloth off the shelf and got it wet it in the warm water and wiped her face ever so gently. He put toothpaste on her toothbrush and let her brush her teeth. While, he held her carefully so she wouldn't hurt herself. After she was done, he took the towel off her head and gently brushed her hair for her. They both just stood there, looking into each other's eyes. It was a fantastic moment. They didn't need words. They could read each other's eyes.

"Do you feel better now?" Harrison asked.

She smiled and moved her body toward him. She put her hands on his face and bent his head down to hers, and then, her lips touched his. His mouth opened and their tongues met. His hands holding her body so close to his body. He was so gentle as if he was scared that he might break her. He kept trying to let her go, but she wouldn't let him. When he tried to break off, she just kissed him deeper, wrapping her arms around him.

"You need to rest so you can get better. I am taking you back to the couch so you can lie down. I'll put on a movie for you," he said. Angelina made a pouting face.

"You promised if I helped you clean up, you would rest afterwards," he said with a smile on his face, and then he helped her to lie down on the couch.

"Thank you for helping me. I feel so much better. I can't wait till the nurse comes on Monday so I can finally take a bath," Angelina admitted.

"What movie do you want to watch?" Harrison asked as he looked at her collection of movies.

"I don't care—whatever you want to watch. You are going to stay with me, aren't you?" she said with hope in her voice. She didn't want him to leave partly because she didn't want to be alone, but mostly because all she wanted was to be with him. He grabbed the movie *Adventures of Love* and put it on for them to watch. He walked over to the chair, sat down, and looked at her.

"Yes, I'll stay as long as you want me to." He replied.

"Will you lie down with me and just hold me while we watch the movie?" She just looked at him hoping that he would say yes.

"I don't think it's a good idea, Angel. I don't want to hurt you. You need to keep your stomach straight so you don't tear your stitches."

She was disappointed, but she knew he really just didn't want to hurt her. They started watching the movie, but that didn't last long as they started talking.

"Can I ask you a question?" She looked at him, waiting for him to answer.

"Yes, what's up?" He answered.

"When I told you that I died and saw my parents, you didn't say anything. Do you believe me?" Angelina asked.

"Well, at first, I wasn't sure what to think, and I was really just so happy you woke up that I really didn't think about it," he said. "Can you tell me what you remember of heaven?"

She told him most of what she could remember and as best as

she could, but there really were no words that existed that could describe her experience.

They talked for hours and hours. He asked questions, and she answered. She cried, and so did he at moments.

Eva called to see if Angelina was feeling up to have dinner with everyone. But she really just wanted to stay with Harrison, so Henry brought dinner up to them. After they ate, Harrison cleaned up, and they watched another movie until Angelina fell asleep on the couch. Harrison picked her up and carried her to her bed. He tucked her in, and as he was going to leave, she pulled his hand.

"Please, will you stay with me and just hold me? I don't want to be alone." she spoke in such a sweet voice, and her eyes looked scared that he couldn't say no to her.

Harrison climbed into bed with her. They faced each other. She leaned in to kiss him, and he backed off. She made a sad face, feeling rejected. He then moved in closer and kissed her forehead.

"Why do you keep doing that? Why don't you want to kiss me? Has something changed?" She was feeling self-conscious. She never really thought about herself as sexy or desirable, but he made her feel that way before, but ever since she woke up, she felt something different.

"Oh my angel, I don't want to hurt you, and we are lying in a bed, and I don't want to get carried away." He touched her face and looked in her eyes; even in the dark, they were so beautiful.

"I'm afraid of moving too fast. I don't want to ruin this. This is all new, and I don't want to scare you."

She didn't say anything after that, she just cuddled in to him, and he held her. Both of them lay there with their eyes open, not talking for a while, then he fell asleep.

It had never occurred to her that kissing on the bed would change things or be different than kissing on the couch. She had never had a boyfriend before, so all of this was so new to her. She had never really thought about sex before, because she was raised as a Catholic, so you don't have sex till you are married. She thought about things, like her parents, but they were not married until after she was born. She didn't really know what she believed or what she wanted. She was falling in love with him, she was sure about that. *But was she ready?* She never really thought about sex much other than in health class. She knew it was going to be something that would come up again. So she would have to make a decision, and she thought it should be something they should talk about. But she was scared and didn't know how to talk about that stuff because it was so embarrassing. So far, their whole relationship had been so intense because of everything that had happened, and because they had known each other for so long and their lives were so involved. As she lay there in his arms, she knew she was in love with him, and there was no way of not getting serious fast because of everything they had been through together. Then she knew what she wanted after everything she had been through. Life is too short to play it safe.

CHAPTER 8

Because of being stuck in her house for a few weeks, Angelina was going crazy. She spent her days on the couch with her laptop. Even though she would ace her finals, because she read all her textbooks and knew all her stuff. She spent her days doing homework so she didn't fall behind.

She had been spending her mornings with Eva and the family and evenings and nights with Harrison. She had been communicating with people by e-mail, and she had received so many letters from people who wanted to hear her story and tell her about their lives.

People that she worked with and some of her classmates stopped by to visit her. So many people were touched by her saving the lives of the children at the community center. Father Patrick had been stopping by to visit her because she hadn't been at church for so long. She always enjoyed her visits with him. He had always been there for her.

Father Patrick told her how so many new people had joined the church since they found out that it was the church of the community center Angel. That is what people were calling her. Father Patrick stopped by on one Thursday afternoon to talk to Angelina. They were both sitting in the living room, having a cup of tea and cookies.

Father Patrick was a very old man with short white hair and very kind, little green eyes. He was very small in stature but had a deep, comforting voice.

"I am so happy to finally be able to get out of this house. I had a doctor's appointment the other day, and I got my stitches removed, and I am healing up really well," Angelina was happy as she told Father Patrick her good news. "I still have to take it easy, so I can't go back to school yet, but soon I will I hope, but I can come to church this Sunday." "Well, that's what I want to talk to you about, you can say no," he said, sipping his tea. "But I would really love it if on Sunday you would speak at church about your experiences of what had happened to you. Your story is amazing, and I know you have always kept everything to yourself. But maybe, sharing your story with others could help people. So what do you think? Will you talk at church on Sunday?"

Angelina had been thinking a lot about sharing her story ever since Dr. Hayford asked her a few months ago. She looked at Father Patrick. He had so much hope in his old face that she didn't want to let him down. He had always been there for her.

"Father, do you believe I went to heaven and saw my parents. Do you believe me?" she asked.

"Oh yes my dear Angelina, I have known you for your whole life. I know you very well. You have never been one for fantasizing and making up stories. I can read your eyes, I know what you saw," he spoke in such a comforting way. Angelina didn't know if she was ready for sharing but she didn't feel like she could so no.

"Yes, I will. I'll tell my story at church. I'll talk about my family and about dying and seeing my parents and about never losing faith, no matter what." She responded.

Father Patrick was so pleased that he clapped his hands with joy and then gave her a hug.

"Thank you so much, my dear. People are going to be so happy to see you," he said as he finished his tea. "I have to get going, but I'll see you on Sunday."

"Yes you will. Have a good day," she said walking Father Patrick to the door. He left her apartment, and then the phone rang. These days it rang a lot. Everyone was always calling her all the time to see how she was doing.

Angelina didn't want to answer the phone; all she wanted to do was lie down on her couch and cry. She got shot, and things were coming back to her. She was feeling scared all the time. She struggled with her own feelings and emotions. She wanted to be alone sometimes, but at the same time, she felt scared. She was having anxiety attacks a lot, and the doctor told her that it was completely normal for someone who had been through a horrific event to have such episodes.

The phone kept ringing and ringing, so she finally answered it.

"Hello, Dr. Hayford," Angelina said looking at caller ID.

"Hello, Angelina, how are you feeling these days?" Dina asked.

"Much better, but I am still taking it easy." Angelina replied.

"Good. I am glad you are feeling better" Dina said. "I have been talking to the school about your placement because of your special circumstances. They have agreed to let you graduate without it, but you need one extra credit."

"OK, well, how would I get an extra credit in less than a month?" Angelina asked concerned.

"Angelina, if you would be interested in telling your story for a few classes that I teach. I will work it out with the school that it would count toward a placement or the extra credit that you need." Dina replied.

Angelina and Dina had been talking every week since she had been home. They had formed a close relationship. She thought about it for a minute. Her whole body started to shake of just the thought of standing in a classroom with her peers. Telling them all her secrets made her whole face go white as if she had seen a ghost.

"Hum." Angelina stammered.

"You don't have to give me an answer today. I know this will be hard for you, but it might be good for you, as well," Dr. Hayford said in an understanding voice.

"Ok I'll do it; I'll talk in about my experiences your classes to get a credit for the placement so I will be able to graduate. But I don't know how much I will be able to get through, and my legs may give out on me, and I will most likely cry." Angelina said.

"That's OK. I am glad you are going to do this," Dina answered.

"Will you fail me if I try and can't get through it all?" Angelina asked.

"No, I will not fail you. Even if you just try, it's an automatic pass." Dina replied.

"OK then, I will try to tell my story. But I still need some more time, I just not ready yet." said Angelina.

"You let me know what day works for you," said Dina. "Take care of yourself and have a great day."

"OK, talk to you soon," Angelina said as she hung up the phone.

That Saturday, Harrison had made plans to take Angelina out on their first official date. It had been a few months since she got shot. She had to take it easy, and she was doing and feeling much better. She was so happy to finally be out of the house; it was really a nice day to be outside.

She got dressed. She had lost a lot of weight over the last few months, so her aunt went out and bought her some new clothes. She put on a really nice gray knit sweater dress and a pair of black tights. She still couldn't wear jeans because her stomach was still so sensitive. She put on a pair of gray flat boots and a jean jacket and put her hair half up. It was the first time she got to where normal clothes and looked and felt good in weeks.

Angelina stood in front of the mirror in her bedroom and stared at herself. She wanted to cry. She looked different. No one had told her she looked different, she couldn't place it herself. But something about her face was not the same. She got up really close and looked into the mirror and looked at her own eyes, and she didn't recognize them. Tears started to build up, and she wiped them away.

Her eyes were normally a very dark brown, but today, they looked like they had little speckles of blue in them. Angelina rubbed her eyes as if she was seeing something that wasn't there. But her eyes really did have little specks of blue in them. She didn't understand why. But she finished getting ready. She had been feeling different since she came back to life, but she just thought it was normal after what she had been through. But as she stood there, looking at herself, she thought she saw herself starting to glow. In that moment, she looked radiantly beautiful, almost like an angel, but then the light was gone, and she looked normal again. Angelina shook her head and thought that maybe she was taking too many pain pills.

Angelina was so excited but was so nervous at the same time. She had butterflies in her tummy and goose bumps on her arms when she heard Harrison at her door. He didn't even knock anymore, because he was there every day.

"So how are you feeling today?" Harrison asked.

She had the biggest smile on her face as she walked into the living room, where he was waiting for her.

"I am feeling really good. I showered and got dressed all by myself, and I'm wearing normal clothes," she said with so much joy in her voice. *After death, you really start to appreciate the little things in life.* "Now, I get to go out and spend the whole day with you. So I am happy,"

"You look very nice today," he said, touching her hand. He was still so gentle with her.

"You look nice, too," she said as she was checking him out. He was wearing dark blue jeans, a white knit sweater, and white running shoes which complemented him very well because of his dark golden skin and dark brown hair and eyes.

"Well, I am all ready to go," she said. She was so excited to get out of the house and to be with him.

"Yes, you are ready, but I told you I have nothing planned until later," he said, laughing.

"That's fine. I don't care what we do today, before our secret date, which you won't tell me about. I just want to get out of the house. We can go to a museum or to a mall or just out for lunch. Anything, please, I don't want to see this apartment at all today." He walked over to her and gave her a sweet gentle kiss, being very careful not to hurt her.

"OK. We will go out all day, but it's your first day out, so we have to take it easy." He said. "She smiled at him, and they walked out of her apartment and went out for the day.

They spent the whole day at the museum. Angelina was fascinated with all the beautiful artwork. She was impressed with how much he knew about the museum.

"This was my mom's favorite place to go in the city. When I was a kid, she would bring me here. She would spend hours telling me all about the artist. I think she wanted me to grow up to be an artist." He smiled, but she could see the heartbreak in his eyes.

She didn't say anything. She just gently touched his hand, letting him know she was there for him. They had a connection she didn't have with anyone else. Maybe, it was because they both shared something horrific in their lives, or maybe it was more.

"I love art. Maybe I got it from my mom, but it's a beautiful way to escape from reality," he said with so much passion in his voice.

They came to a beautiful sculpture of a woman holding a baby in her arms it was simple but magnificent; the beauty of a mother and her love for her child was beyond amazing. They both just looked at the statue and held each other's hands real tight. They both had a moment when tears came to their eyes, but they breathed through it.

Angelina thought about the beautiful angelic woman she saw in heaven—her mother. She shut her eyes and wanted to feel her mother's love just for a moment. In her mind she heard that song, the one her mother sang the day she died. As Angelina started to shake, she felt a warm embrace of love come all around her, and she knew that it was her mother's love, giving her strength and courage and letting her know she was loved.

"Thank you for bringing me here and sharing this special place with me," she said as they were leaving the museum.

They walked up the streets of Toronto until they came to a small Italian restaurant. "This is the place," he said with big happy eyes. He looked like a child on his birthday opening up his gifts. They walked inside, and they were met by an older man wearing a blue suit. The man looked overjoyed to see Harrison. He shook his hand and kissed his cheeks in the way Italians do.

"Harrison, I am so pleased that you have come here for dinner. I have missed you so much. It has been too long," the old man said, like he was choking back tears.

"You are not the same boy I remember. You are a man now, and I see you have a beautiful girlfriend," the little man said with a strong Italian accent.

Angelina smiled and said thank you with her eyes as her face lit up with joy.

"Yes, I am sorry it's been so long. I just didn't think I could come back to this place, but I am happy that I am here now," Harrison said, smiling and still holding her hand. She could feel that his palms were sweaty and he held her hand so tightly.

"Angelina, this is Tony. He owns this restaurant, and he was one of my parents' best friends. This is Angelina, my girlfriend and neighbor," Harrison introduced them. The man kissed her hand.

"I'll show you to your table," the man said as he led the way.

The restaurant was small but busy. It was dark but had a romantic feel to it. The décor was dark grays and blues and had beautiful artwork on the walls. They sat down at their table, and the man poured them both a glass of white wine.

"Your restaurant is beautiful. I love all the artwork on the walls," Angelina said to the man. He smiled at her, and then he looked at Harrison, who was shaking his head.

"Thank you. They were all painted by him," Tony said, pointing at Harrison.

Angelina was shocked. She didn't know that he was an artist. All his work was so beautiful that she didn't have words to describe how amazing they were. Her face lit up with joy, and her eyes looked so happy. They were almost glowing.

"Wow how impressive!" Angelina smiled as she sipped her wine.

"So your mom's dream did come true, you are an artist. Your artwork is incredible." She smiled at him with joy in her eyes, and he couldn't help but smile back. His face lit up with happiness just from looking at her beautiful face. He was so much in love with her.

CHAPTER 9

The waiter brought them chicken parmesan on a bed of pasta. It looked and smelt amazing. She could smell the garlic and peppers; the first bite was succulent.

"I think this is the best food I have ever had," Angelina said, smiling as she took another bite.

"I know. This is my favorite restaurant. I haven't been here in years, but I am so glad that I am here with you now." Harrison replied.

After their amazing dinner, they said good-bye to Tony and went off to the next activity.

"Are you feeling all right? Because we can take a cab to the theater," he said, putting his arm around her as they walked down the street.

"I am just fine with walking," she said and smiled at him with excitement on her face.

"So, we are going to the theater. What are we going to see?"

she asked. He had a disappointed look on his face that he let it slip out; he wanted it to be a surprise.

"It's a surprise," he said in a nervous way. She wanted to reassure him that she was happy and wanted to be with him.

"I am having such a good time," she said, looking up into his big brown eyes. They were like a black hole which sucked her in. She could get lost just looking into his eyes.

They walked into the theater and found their seats. The room was very large and had a balcony. There must have been hundreds of people in the room. The stage was covered with big dark red curtains. The room was dark, even though there were so many lights everywhere.

Angelina was so excited. She didn't know what they were going to see, but the whole experience was so new and fun to her. He watched her looking around the room with excitement in her eyes.

"We're going to see "*Love the Opera*," he whispered in her ear. He watched her more than he watched the show. He took pleasure in seeing her face light up with excitement.

When they were walking to their apartment building, hand in hand, they were both very quiet. It was a nice night—not too cold and the lights of the city cast a romantic feel as they walked.

"Thank you for today. This was the best date." She smiled. He could see how happy she was. "I pictured today in my head all week, and it was so much better than I imagined it to be. I am so happy. I can't believe you took me to see an opera. It was incredible, I loved it."

"I am so happy you had a good time. When I was thirteen, and started liking girls, I asked my mom what was the best date she had ever been on. She told me it was when my dad took her out to her favorite Italian restaurant and then to the opera. So I hoped that you would think it as special as my mom did," he said, then looked at her with his big eyes full of joy.

"I think that story made this day even better. It was so great. I loved it," she said as they walked into their apartment building.

"I promised you that you wouldn't have to see your apartment today. So I was thinking we could stay at my place tonight." She looked a little nervous.

"Yes we can do that."

Harrison's place was pretty much the same layout as Angelina's but just one bedroom, and it was a little smaller and didn't have a fireplace. The living/dining room combination walls were a light blue. He had a small glass table with only two chairs in the dining area. Two small black leather futons were his couches and he had a big flat-screen TV on a little black stand. Paintings covered the walls and an easel and paint stand was in the corner.

She walked in and realized she had never really been in his apartment much. She saw all the paintings and they took her breath away. She was fascinated with the way he saw the world. His pictures were incredible.

"Wow, all this artwork is beautiful! Did you do all of these?" smiling as she asked.

"Yes, I just love painting. It's just for fun, a hobby, a little fun thing I do," he replied.

"So all those paintings you have given to Aunt Eva and to me over the years were painted by you? I didn't know that. I am so impressed."

She was looking around at all the paintings, and then she came to a big one on the floor, and she held it up to look at it. She was shocked. It brought tears to her eyes.

She looked at Harrison. He put his head down like he was embarrassed. The painting was phenomenal; it took her breath away. It was her face, but she was glowing. It was in black and white. She looked like an Angel.

"Wow! This is me." She had tears in her eyes. She was overwhelmed with the way he saw her. It made her feel so special.

"Yes this is how I see you. I am sorry. I hope that doesn't freak you out. It's just when you were in the hospital. I didn't know if you would wake up, so I wanted to remember how beautiful you are, and I just had to paint." He looked away from her, like he was scared of her response.

"I look so beautiful in your eyes. Wow! It's amazing! I love it." She felt overwhelmed but yet she was so touched.

"You are beautiful. Every person who has ever met you

knows how pretty you are, everyone but you," he spoke about her with so much energy and passion.

He grabbed her hand and took her to the couch and turned on some music. He went to the kitchen and got a bottle of wine and two glasses. They both had a glass of wine and sat on the futon, looking into each other's eyes.

"Every time, I think this day can't get any better, it does. Thank you for being my best friend. You are so amazing to me. You have made my life so much better," she said while sipping some of her wine and looking at him with a smile on her face.

"I feel the same way about you. I think you are amazing, and I am totally in love with you." He said then he looked shocked and scared.

The words fell out of his mouth. It was like the most beautiful song to her ears. She knew he loved her. She could see it in his eyes, read it off in his face, feel it in his touch, and she felt the same way. She was euphorically and unconditionally overjoyed by the love she felt.

"I know it's way too early to say that, but life is too short, and I don't want to miss my chance to tell you how I feel. I don't want to freak you out by moving too fast. But I am so in love with you," he said very nervously.

She had tears in her eyes. She leaned into him, starring into his eyes. She touched his face. She started kissing him, and this time, he didn't stop her. He put the futon down so they could be more comfortable. His hands were all over her body, but he was moving slowly and gently. As his lips were on her neck, he was trying to control his passion, and she whispered in his ear, "I am in love with you, too."

He stopped and looked into her eyes, touching her face. He kissed her. It was strong but sweet. They kissed for a long time, and then they just lay there, looking at each other.

"Angelina, are you OK? You are shaking." He asked her while holding her in his arms.

"I am fine. I am just a little nervous. I am so happy. Right now, everything is perfect. I don't want anything to change. In my life, nothing good ever lasts a long time," she said in such a sweet voice with an innocent look on her face.

"Nothing has to change, my Angel. Don't worry. I love you, and I am not going anywhere."

She yawned, and then so did he. They both got up and went to the bedroom. He gave her a t-shirt to sleep in. They got into his bed and lied there, just looking at each other so happy. She fell asleep with him holding her; it was her safe, happy place—his arms.

The next morning, there was a very loud knock at the door. They both got up and went into the living room. Eva was standing in the door way. Harrison answered the door, not wearing a shirt, and Angelina was standing there, wearing his t-shirt and with no pants on. Eva put her hands on her hip.

"You two need to be ready to go to church in twenty minutes.

Angelina, you are speaking today, remember?" Eva had this concerned look on her face, but her voice sounded angry.

"Sorry, Aunt Eva, we overslept. We will be ready in twenty minutes," Harrison said, shutting the door, but Eva just glared at Angelina like she had committed a sin. The door shut.

Angelina stood there frozen for a moment, she took a deep breath. They both looked at each other and laughed, and he walked over to her and gave her a big hug, which made her feel happy again.

"Well, we better get ready to go before we get into big trouble," he said, laughing.

Angelina went to her apartment and got dressed and looked at herself in the mirror. She took a deep breath. "You can do this. Everyone has a purpose on earth and in heaven, maybe this is your purpose—to share your story and give people hope that there is more after we die," She grabbed her bag and walked out of the door.

CHAPTER 10

There must have been at least a thousand people in St. Mary's church that Sunday. It had never been that busy before, but so many people came to hear Angelina's story. Her family sat in the front row. She sat there anxiously, waiting to give her speech. She was holding Harrison's hand so tightly. He whispered in her ear, "You are going to get through this. You're going to be amazing. You are going to help people believe in something they want to believe in so badly. It's going to be OK. You can do this." She looked in his eyes, and she could feel his love. She smiled with the most nervous look on her face.

Angelina got up to the top of the church and spoke into the microphone. She was shaking. Her heart was beating so fast that she was sure the person in the back row could hear it. She shut her eyes and took a deep breath, and it was like she could feel her father's presence, like he was there, giving her the strength to speak. All her anxiety disappeared, and she spoke clearly and with confidence.

"Hello, everyone, I am so honored that you are all interested in hearing my story. I want to thank all of you for all your prayers. I am doing and feeling much better these days with the help of my family. Well, I am Angelina Heart, and to tell my story, I have to start from when I was young. I had the best childhood. I had the greatest parents. They loved me so much, and we were so happy. When I was five years old, just weeks before Christmas, there was a bank robbery at the bank where my dad worked. There were about twenty-six people left in the bank that day, and it was about twenty minutes before the bank closed. I was playing in the playhouse, when four men came in to rob the bank. Twenty-four people made it out alive that day, but my parents weren't in the group that survived. I remember being very scared and seeing a lot of blood, and I didn't understand why my parents had to die." Tears fell down her face, but she didn't break focus. She kept speaking.

"I lived with my grandma for a year after that until she got sick and died. I was sitting in the hospital room with her. I was six when, for the second time, someone I loved died in front of me. I lived with my aunt Jenny for a couple of years, and then, Jenny and I were going to move into my uncle John and Aunt Eva's apartment building. The day we moved, John, Jenny, and I were on our way to our new house, and we were hit by a bus. I was nine years old. I woke up all alone in a hospital room; most of my bones were broken. Father Patrick, who had been a friend of my family for my whole life and who helped me when my parents died, came to visit me. He was the one who told me that Jenny and John had gone to heaven to be with my mom and dad and grandma. That was the first time I questioned my faith. Why did God hate me so much that he kept taking away everyone I loved? I wanted to live in heaven with God, too. Why was I still here all alone? Father Patrick told me God loved me and that he just wasn't ready for me yet. So there I was, nine, and all my blood relatives were gone. Aunt Eva took me in to live with her. She cared for me as I was her daughter. She helped me and supported me through everything. My teen years were hard. I didn't have many friends because I was scared of what people would think of me, so I pushed people away. I made it through college with my nose in books, learning, and my faith in God. That is what has always helped me through everything. My life was going pretty good. I was a university psych student, I had just started dating for the first time in my life, and I was happy." She smiled.

"That day, I went to school. I went to work at the community center. I was working in the youth program. We were in the gym, playing basketball when a gang of teens came in and threatened my kids. I hope no one takes offence at me referring to the teens as my kids, but I love what I do, and I love the kids I work with. When I work and help get these kids on the right track, it helps me to be a better person. It gives me hope. The leader of the gang told me that three of my kids were to leave with him or he would kill them. He showed me his gun. One of the guys I was working with called the police. My plan was to stall the gang. Talk to the kids until the police showed up. I had dealt with gangs before, so I didn't think things were going to get as bad as they did. Once I realized no matter what I did something bad was going to happen,

I got scared. I knew we had to try to get some of the kids out of the gym as fast as we could.

"I distracted the gang of boys by talking to them, while the two male staff I was working with, snuck the kids out of the gym. But then, things got bad. One child was standing alone unprotected, and I saw the boy with the gun take aim at him. Honestly, I can't explain what I was feeling or even thinking. It all happened so fast. All I knew was I had to protect that little boy. That was all that mattered to me. I didn't think about anything else. I ran to him, hoping that when I covered him, the boy would put the gun down and I could help him, but it was too late. I heard a loud bang, and then I was on the ground, and the cops were there. I was in so much pain. I remember seeing that little boy's face looking at me with tears in his eyes as he held my hand. I was so happy that he was not harmed. I didn't even care about anything else at that moment. The pain was unbearable. I remember a paramedic talking to me, but then, I shut my eyes. It was all dark, and then I didn't feel any more pain.

"Then there was light and warmth and the most beautiful music I had ever heard, but it was sung by birds. When I finally opened my eyes, I didn't really know where I was, and I didn't know how or why I was there. It was so magnificent, and the love that I felt was amazing. It was like I was in a meadow, with flowers and babbling brooks, but it was as if it was on top of the clouds. I saw the most beautiful angelic woman. She came to me, and it was the most amazing experience. It was my mother. I held her in my arms so tight because I didn't want to let her go, and then, I saw my father. It was the most amazing family reunion

I could have ever dreamed. We didn't have to say a word. We could feel what each other felt. I was so happy. I saw my aunt and uncle. They all look so joyful and perfect, more beautiful than I remembered them to be. There were lots of people I didn't know. I think they were like me—new to that place. I thought I was in heaven because how could anything be better than where I was. That's when I saw the different ways into heaven. I always thought there would be a gateway to Heaven, but there was more than one way in. There was a river that led to a big castle. It was enchanting to look at, so astonishing. There was a staircase that appeared to move. I think that's where the angels get their wings. I also saw the most beautiful shining gates, and inside, the light was so bright, and all I could feel was so much love and happiness. I was hoping I got to go in there, but then, a part of me started missing the people in my life. I knew I was not supposed to be there yet. If I was, I wouldn't still feel attached to earth. I remember looking at my family, because I also wanted to stay with them forever, but now I know they will be there, waiting for me. I remember it felt like I was floating back into my body. I heard a heartbeat and that's what brought me back." With tears falling down her face, she kept looking at Harrison.

"People have asked me how I feel about the people who killed my parents. I know they ruined their own lives and also the lives of the people they love. Everything we do is a choice, and we make decisions every day that will affect our lives later on. Those people made a bad choice ruining so many lives, including their own. As for the boy that shot me, I wish I could have done more to help him. Before he hurt me, I don't wish bad things to him, but I also know that jail can't be fun. My advice for people is *live*. Please, make good choice, but have fun. Go to school, travel, work hard, have good friends, treat people with respect, fall in love, be true to yourself, and never lose faith in God and in who you are." Tears were pouring out of her eyes, she couldn't stop them, but in some way, she felt amazing. It was nice—getting everything out. She felt special and important that so many people cared to take the time to listen to her story.

After church, so many people were talking to Angelina. Some people cried listening to her story. Church was done at eleven, but they were there until after two, talking to people. Angelina and her aunt went out together for a coffee and to talk. Henry, Harrison, and the twins went home.

CHAPTER 11

Eva and Angelina spent all afternoon at a local coffee house chatting and drinking cappuccinos.

"So, Angelina, why did you want to get away, just the two of us," Eva asked, looking at Angelina curiously.

"I thought it would be nice for us to just hang out and talk. You seemed really mad this morning when you found me in Harrison's apartment. So I thought maybe we needed sometime together." Angelina said.

"I was not mad. I was just caught off guard. He is my nephew, and you are my niece, and this is really different for me. I am happy for you two, and I know he will treat you good. And I also know he couldn't find a better girl, but it's still weird for me," she said in a sweet voice. She was worried; Angelina could tell by the look in her eyes. "Then I saw you two this morning half naked, and I was just surprised. I know you both are adults and you can do whatever you want to. I am just scared that you two are moving really fast, and if this doesn't work out"—Eva took a sip of her coffee—"I am family to both of you, and I can't take sides," Eva said, looking at her with those mothering eyes.

"I understand. That makes sense. But I died. And more than anyone, I know that life can change forever, at any moment," She spoke with so much intensity in her voice. "I have never been this happy, and we are moving so fast because, yes, we have just started dating. But we are already in love with each other. We have known each other for so long, and we have been through so much together. We can't help it, maybe, when it's right, you just know because it feels so right," she said as she looked at her aunt, hoping for her support.

"Seeing you like this is so much fun. I need to stop worrying about you so much. I keep forgetting that you are not sixteen but twenty-four. When I was your age, I was already married for two years. I can't believe you just said you are in love." Her aunt smiled and laughed a little bit.

"Yeah, well, I am, and I never planned this. I really don't have many girlfriends, so you are really the one I have to talk to, considering I am dating my best friend." She smiled with a funny look on her face.

"You want to talk to me about sex, don't you?" Eva said, laughing, finishing up her coffee. Angelina had this helpless look on her face.

"I am just scared, and I don't know what I am doing," Angelina said, all embarrassed.

"It's like you said, when its right you just know it is right," Eva said.

They continued talking all afternoon as they walked home. They both enjoyed their time together. They needed that time to just sit and talk and laugh.

Angelina went back to school; everyone was so happy to see her. The last few weeks of school flew by. Angelina shared her story for Dina Hayford's classes and received credits toward a placement, so she was able to graduate with her classmates. Angelina was happy to be back in school, even if it was just for the last few weeks. She wasn't back to work yet, and she didn't know what her next plan would be, now that school was almost done.

She was going around, doing a lot of public speaking and even talking on some local radio stations, telling her story. People all over Toronto knew about her as the community center Angel. She received so many thank you cards from so many people, telling her how her story helped them through bad things in their lives. Both she and Harrison graduated on the same weekend in June. Eva held a graduation party for them.

Eva's apartment was very large, and it was all decorated beautifully with candles everywhere, and all the party decorations were blue and white. Everyone was dressed up, looking their best. Eva made Angelina get her hair done and made Harrison get his cut. She even bought them new clothes to wear at the party.

Harrison wore a baggie suit with a black golf shirt, and Angelina had her hair up in curls, and she was wearing a gold lace dress that went just past her knees and had a black sash around her waist. They completed each other so perfectly. So many people came to the party; ever since Angelina came back to life, she was more open to befriending people.

Harrison had a lot of friends at school as well and it was nice for Angelina to meet Harrison's friends. They were both so happy. Harrison introduced Angelina to his best friend.

"This is my girlfriend Angelina. And this is my best friend Matthew from school and this is his girlfriend Gwen," Harrison said, as Angelina shook Matthew's and Gwen's hands.

"It's so nice to meet both of you." Angelina was excited to be introduced as his girlfriend.

Matt was a short guy with a solid physic. He looked a lot younger than Harrison. He had red hair and green eyes. Gwen was very pretty. She was taller than Mathew. She was thin and had golden-blonde hair up to her shoulders and hazel color eyes.

"Nice to meet you too, Harrison never stops talking about you," Matt said and then he left to go talk to some other people.

"I didn't know you were such a popular guy, I always thought you were kind of a dork." she said, laughing at him.

"Oh really? Well, that's OK, because I think you are a dork, too." He laughed as he kissed her, and then they both went off to mingle with the people.

There were about five girls that were talking to Angelina,

telling her stories about Harrison. She felt uncomfortable, because the girls were judging her for some reason; they kept looking at her every time she moved with negative eyes.

"You are pretty lucky to be dating Harrison," said a girl with long beautiful red hair. She was tall and thin and very attractive. "I asked him out like seven times, but he always turned me down," she said, looking at Angelina like there was something wrong with her.

Angelina didn't know how to respond to that, so she didn't say anything; she just stood there, listening to the girls' talk.

"He was one of the nicest and best looking guys in our school," a short girl with curly short brown hair said. She was sweet looking but not as pretty as the other girls.

"Yeah, I was the only girl Harrison ever dated at school," said a beautiful blonde girl. She was also tall and curvy. She had big lips and big blue eyes and a she had a cruel look on her face like Angelina had stolen him from her. But she still didn't say anything. "He blew me off, so I would consider myself lucky if I were you," the girl said with jealousy in her voice, they all laughed with her.

Angelina was feeling uncomfortable, and then a pair of arms wrapped around her waist; it was Harrison. She felt calm and safe.

"The truth is I am the lucky one," he said, looking each one of the girls in their eyes, and then he pulled her away from all the girls.

She was so relieved and happy that he saved her from them, she didn't know how to handle girls like that.

They stayed together for the rest of the party. When it was time for toasts, everyone had something to say. Henry spoke first; of course, he always had to have the first and the last word.

"I want to say thank you to everyone for coming and celebrating with us today. I want to send out a big congratulations to all the graduates here tonight." Some of them shouted and cheered. "Now, Harrison, your aunt and I are so very proud of you for all your accomplishments. You have been through a lot, and it has helped you become the man you are today. Your parents would be so happy and proud of you, just like we are proud of you. Now, I know I am not your father, but I love you like a son." Henry had tears in his eyes as he concluded his speech, and everyone cheered.

"Now to the beautiful Angel of the family: this has been a hard year, and just a few months ago, we didn't know if you would be alive to celebrate today. But you, being the strongest girl I have ever met, fought to be alive. You are amazing. You are truly a beautiful person. Congratulations! All your hard work is paying off. I know you are not sure what your next move is going to be in life. But we know whatever you do, it will be amazing. I wish you all the happiness and success, because that's what you deserve. We will always be here to support you, because we love you. Now everyone raise a glass to Harrison and Angelina. Congratulations!" Everyone cheered. Harrison and Angelina went up and gave Henry a hug.

Eva spoke. She had tears in her eyes even before she started. "I'm not going to say a lot, because I will just cry even more. I am so proud of both of you. Any parent would be so lucky to have a son as friendly and sweet and as understanding as you are, Harrison. I am so proud of the man you have grown up to be. Any mother would be so lucky to have a daughter like you, Angelina. You truly are my Angel, always helping people, no matter what. Angelina, you are sweet, understanding, nonjudgmental, and so very smart and generous. There isn't anything you wouldn't do to help someone else. I am so proud of the person you have become and so pround of all your accomplishments. I know both of your parents are looking down at you both today. They would be so proud of the people you have become, and I am so happy that you two have each other to share all your joy with," Eva said, with tears running down her face as she starred at Angelina. She was crying too. She loved her aunt so much; she helped her to become everything she was. She was so touched by all the beautiful things she had said. Angelina and Eva were both so emotional and they all hugged for a long time.

After that, more people got up and talked about both of them. Harrison's friends talked about how he helped them over the years. Many people got up and talked about Angelina being such an inspiration. After all their classmates had spoken, Angelina spoke, she was so excited and joyful.

"I have to go before Harrison does, because I'm sure he will make me cry. I am so touched by everything you all had to say. I never knew so many people thought so many nice things about me. I am so happy that we have finally graduated from school.

It's funny how you all think of me as an inspiration, because I wouldn't be the person I am today if it wasn't for the people in my life. Aunt Eva, I am who I am because you raised me this way. I am grateful for everything you have ever done for me. I love you so much, and you are a mom to me," she spoke with so much love in her voice that her eyes were glowing with internal happiness.

"Thank you to my classmates, you needed my help to study and stuff made me to do my best so that I could help all of you. Henry, thank you for always telling me that you believed in me. My father passed away when I was so young, it has been nice to have you in my life." She smiled at Henry, who had tears in his eyes.

"Father Patrick, thank you for always guiding me and helping me to make the right choices. Thank you for supporting me spiritually and emotionally. I am so happy to have you in my life." Angelina smiled at Father Patrick.

"Harrison, it's hard for me to say this, but if I had of died a week earlier, I don't think I would have woken up." Tears started building up in her eyes, and her voice cracked, but she fought through her emotions and kept talking. "I came back for you, because I am so in love with you." She found his eyes and starred at him the whole time she talked. "It's funny, but I believe some things are meant to happen. I don't know why it took us so long to get together, but I am so unbelievably happy to have you in my life. You make me so happy, and I am so proud of all your accomplishments. I know how hard you worked to get to where you are today. I don't know what the future holds, but I believe we are supposed to be in each other's lives, always. Thank you to everyone for coming to celebrate with us. Here's to the future, may it be happy and fulfilling," she said as she raised her glass, and everyone cheered. She kissed Harrison and then went and gave her friends and family hugs.

Then Harrison began to talk. "Well, I think it's my turn to speak, but I don't know how I can top any of that. I am so happy to be here today; finally we are all college graduates it feels like it took forever. No more school, it is great! I wish my parents were here today, because I know they would be so proud that I graduated again and happy that I found the most amazing girl. I have had hard times in my life, but I have been very fortunate, too. I have Aunt Eva and Henry that gave me a place to live and welcomed me into their family, no questions asked. Thank you for all your support. I love you both so very much. Thanks to all my friends at school, for always bugging me and pushing me to do better. Thank you to my Angel. You have saved me time and time again more than you could ever know." Angelina remembered what the Angel in heaven told her. She understood what Harrison was talking about, but that was her secret.

"You have taught me that no matter what happens in your life, you fight for who you are and what you want, and no matter what happens, never lose faith. Every time in the last five years when I lost faith, in myself or in God and was ready to give up on life, you were always there to guide me in the right direction. Just by being who you are, my best friend. You have the most beautiful heart. You make people better just because they know you. After everything you have been through in your life, you still believe that the world is a beautiful place and that people are beautiful. You make the world beautiful. I love you so much, and I also believe that some things are meant to be. I am so lucky to have you in my life."

Angelina hugged and kissed Harrison. She was emotional and excited and happier than she could remember ever being. She didn't want to let him go. She was overwhelmed by all the love she felt.

When the party was almost over, Henry made an announcement. He and Eva were so excited.

"Angelina and Harrison, for your graduation gift, your aunt and I are taking you both to Cuba in the fall with us for a family vacation."

"Wow, that's amazing!" Angelina and Harrison exclaimed almost in synch.

Everyone was so excited for them. They all cheered. When the party was over, Eva made Harrison and Angelina leave. She wouldn't let them help cleaning up.

CHAPTER 12

Harrison and Angelina left the party and went back to Angelina's cozy little apartment. They were both so tired but so excited they didn't go bed. Angelina hopped into the shower to get all the hair spray out of her hair. She wore a white nightgown and brushed her long brown hair. When she came out of the bathroom, Harrison had candles burning in the living room and two glasses of wine sitting on the coffee table. He had no shirt on, only a pair of PJ pants, and he was sitting on the couch. She walked over and sat on the couch beside him. She fell into his arms and rested her head against his perfectly chiseled chest. He took a glass of wine and handed it to her.

"Today was really nice. I didn't think I would like having a party, but it was fun," she said, laughing as she thought about the night.

"Yes, it was fun and emotional. I didn't expect to cry so much," he said, kind of embarrassed.

"Now we have to decide what to do with the rest of our lives," she said annoyed that she had no clue what lay next for her.

"Well, as long as we get to figure things out together, that will work for me," Harrison said, touching her face and smiling.

"Well, we don't have to make any decisions tonight. For now, let's just enjoy being graduates," she smiled.

She was yawning when he looked down at her. She finished her wine and put the glass on the table.

"Let's go to bed. It's been a long day," he said.

She was tired but didn't want to go bed, but she followed him anyway. They walked into the bedroom, and she grabbed his hand and brought him close to her. She moved her body into his. She bent his head down to hers, and her lips found his. Her hands were all over his body, within seconds, his hands were on her body, too. He was kissing her back so passionately. Then her nightgown fell onto the floor. They just kept kissing. Then they made it to the bed. He paused for a moment to look into her eyes, and he brushed her hair off her face. They both didn't say anything; they didn't have to say a word. She started kissing his neck, and his hands were all over her body again. He was so gentle and loved her so much. Everything was perfect.

They just lay there in each other's arms, looking into each other's eyes with so much love, they were both so unbelievably happy.

"I have something I want to give you. I know I should wait for a while, but I just can't, and I am a little scared, but today has just been so.... Well, I'll be right back," Harrison said, jumping of the bed and running out of the room. He was so excited just like a child.

Angelina stayed lying in her bed. She was so full of joy and love. It was the happiest moment she could ever remember feeling. Harrison came back into the bedroom and got into the bed with her. He was shaking and was so nervous. She didn't understand why he was acting this way.

"I was going to wait until September and give you this on your birthday. But I don't want to wait. Life is too short, right?" he said.

"Yes, life is short." Angelina replied.

"So we shouldn't waste a moment, right?" he asked.

"Sure, we should live as much as we can, you're making me nervous. What's going on?" she asked watching him bounce on the bed from being so nervous and hyper.

"I bought this for you, because both of our birthdays are in September, and I know your mom's was too, so I hope you like it," he said, his eyes were glowing with happiness, but she could tell that he was nervous. His whole face was pale, and his voice was shaky when he spoke.

He pulled out a little blue box that had a little white bow on it. He opened the little box, and inside was a white gold ring with a big round blue sapphire with two rows of diamonds on either side.

Angelina didn't know what to say or to think. She was euphorically happy and so in love with him. Her heart was beating so fast, and her body felt numb. She felt her blood rushing to her face and she felt light headed. At that moment she felt weightless, as if she could float away on a cloud. Never in her life had things been so good. She was overjoyed and overwhelmed that she didn't say anything. She just looked into his eyes, and she was lost and consumed by her love for him.

He didn't get down on one knee, he didn't have some fancy speech, it was just simple and from the heart, and it was true.

"I want to spend the rest of my life loving you. If you feel the same way, accept this ring as a symbol of our love and agree to marry me."

She had tears building up in her eyes. She couldn't believe that so many good things were happening in her life. She put her hand out, and he placed the ring on her left hand.

"Yes I want to marry you, because I know we are meant to be together." Angelina responded. "It was simple and sweet and everything she wanted it to be.

She stared kissing him again. They were both so happy. Nothing mattered at that moment, but there love for each other. Life was too short to worry about tomorrow; tonight they were happy and in love.

"I hope you like it. I wanted to do something different than just a diamond. Everyone gives diamonds. This is special, because it's both of our birthstones, and then I know it would be perfect when you told me your mom's ring had sapphires in it," Harrison spoke while holding her hand and looking down at the ring on her finger. It meant so much to her that it was a sapphire like her mother's was. It made her feel special that her ring was different from most girls' engagement rings yet similar to her mother's.

"It is perfect. I love it. But how could you afford it? You are a college student and you don't have a job," she asked confused and worried that he maxed out his credit card or something like that.

"Well, it's kind of a secret, but my parents were wealthy people. Both my mom and dad were doctors. When they died, they left me a lot of money. So that's how I paid for school and living expenses without having a part-time job. Most of the money is put away so I don't blow through it, but I have more than enough to live off. We can have an amazing wedding and a fabulous honeymoon and a very happy life together." He looked at her with a funny expression on his face and he smiled.

"Yes, my parents had life insurance too," Angelina said. "They left me a little bit of money, but Eva had to use it to take care of me. She was all alone, and she didn't make lots of money. I think I have some money left. Eva put it away for my future. It may be enough for a down payment on a house or something," as she looked at Harrison and she kissed him again.

She got off the bed and turned on the light in the room so

she could see how beautiful her ring was. She was so excited; she had never felt that way before.

"I just want to look at my ring. It is so amazing. Look how beautiful it is," she said in a happy voice as she flashed him her ring with a big smile on her face.

He laughed at her and then he pulled her close and kissed her. She turned off the light and lay in his arms until she fell asleep.

"I love you, always," he whispered in her ear as she dozed off.

Then next day, they stayed in bed all day. She made breakfast, and they ate in bed. What a lovely day! It was so nice for them to just lie in each other's arms, loving each moment of just being together.

"You know, we are going to have to tell Aunt Eva and Henry. I'm a little scared," Harrison said to her, and she felt the same way.

"I know this has all happened fast, but I think they will support us. But we should decide something's before we talk to them about it," Angelina replied.

"Yes, we should, how long do you want to wait, a year? Do you want a big wedding or a small wedding? What kind of flowers do you want? What colors would you like?" he asked. She looked at him and laughed; it was funny how much he wanted to get involved.

"Well, it's up to you, but I would like a small church wedding. I would love Father Patrick to marry us at our church. He married my parents in that church, and it would mean so much to me if we could get married there too. I would like a simple and small wedding and reception for friends and family, nothing big but still elegant and classic. I love white lilies and blues would be a nice color. But I don't want to wait long. I would like to get married soon if that would be OK with you," she responded gleefully as she was getting excited now.

Angelina didn't see the need to wait. Yes, they had only been together for a few months. But she knew that it was right because she could feel that they were meant to be together.

"That all sounds perfect to me. So we should make plans to have dinner with Eva and Henry and even with Father Patrick soon." Harrison said.

She leaned over on top of him and kissed his soft lips, sweet and gentle. "That all can wait for another day, all I want to do right now is stay in this bed all day long and be with you," she said in a sweet yet seductive voice then she kissed him again.

"That works for me." He laughed and kissed her back.

CHAPTER 13

Weeks passed and Angelina had been putting off telling her family that she and Harrison were engaged. Eva knew something was up, because Angelina had been acting odd and distant lately. She had arranged a family dinner at Antonio's Italian restaurant, where Harrison took her on their first date.

Angelina was a bundle of nerves that day. She felt anxious and she was full of giggles. She felt scared and happy all at the same time. She picked out the perfect outfit to wear for dinner. She found a really nice blue top. She would pair it with black dress pants that would look good, and the blue top matched her ring so perfectly. She was so excited. The ring was the most beautiful ring she had ever seen. She couldn't believe it was on her finger. She was so overjoyed and overwhelmed, because getting married was never something she every really thought about before. But now that it was happening, she was so unbelievably and uncontrollably happy. She was going to marry the best man she had ever met. Her excitement was shining out of her. She got ready and cleaned up her apartment. Angelina was alone that afternoon, so she just did things around her apartment.

When she was cleaning, she found things that belonged to her parents. She pulled out her parents wedding book and looked at it. She had a warm happy feeling come over her whole body as she opened the book. Her mother was so beautiful. She was wearing an ivory lace dress with long lace sleeves and a matching veil. Angelina thought she would like something very similar to what her mother's dress looked like. Her mother looked so happy. Angelina could see all the joy and love in her eyes. Her father had that same look on his face; he was overjoyed to marry her mother. He was wearing a pale gray suit with a baby-blue shirt, and he looked so handsome. She flipped the page and came to a picture of all three of them. She was such a cute flower girl with a pretty baby blue dress. It made her cry. It broke her heart over and over again that when something good happened in her life, her parents weren't there to share in her joy.

As a tear feel down her face she remembered the look in her father's eyes and she remember how he was always there. He never missed a moment and as much as she wished she could see him and here him, she took comfort in knowing that he was there with her always.

Angelina was looking at the book, just sitting on the couch when Harrison came in and sat down beside her. He could see she had been crying and he started looking at the pictures with her.

"This was my parents wedding book," she said with a crack

in her voice and she smiled. She didn't look at him. She just kept looking at the pictures.

"Wow! Your mom was so beautiful, and you look just like her," he said, touching her face. She smiled with tears in her eyes.

"Thank you. I don't see it, but thanks, anyway. I loved to think I look like my mother," she said, with more tears falling as she gently rubbed her finger over the picture of her parents. "I love my mom's dress. I think I would like something like that," she said looking at him for a reaction, but he just flipped the pages to see a picture of her.

"Wow! Look how cute you were," he smiled, and his face looked so happy. She smiled and flipped the page to a picture of her with her parents. He could tell she was emotional, so he made a joke, "I love your dad's suit. I think I might wear one just like it for our wedding." He had a smile on his face, and they both laughed.

"Yeah right, I don't think so." She said joking and laughing at him. She flipped the page to a big group picture of her whole family, and she got emotional again. She closed the book. He gave her a hug. They just sat there on the couch and talked for a while.

Everyone met for dinner at the restaurant around the same time as it wasn't far from their apartment building. Eva, Henry, and the twins and Henry's parents Mr. and Mrs. Smoother who were in town for the summer. Both Harrison and Angelina were close with Henry's family. They lived in Toronto in the summer and lived in Florida in the winter.

Father Patrick came, and Harrison's friend Matthew from school came with his girlfriend Gwen. Eva's best friend Helen came. Angelina had known her ever since she was a little girl. Angelina was acting very funny. Everyone could tell something was up. She kept trying to hide her hand; she was clumsy, she kept knocking things over and she was shaking. She didn't want anyone to see the ring until they were ready to tell everyone that they were engaged. Harrison introduced Matthew to Henry's parents. He had already met Angelina and her family at the graduation party.

"Yes, it's too bad that you and mom couldn't have made it in earlier so you could have been here for Angelina and Harrison's graduation," Henry said, looking at his parents.

"Yes, we are very sorry. We were unable to make it to either of your graduations. But we are very happy for both of you. Congrats! So do either of you have any plans for work yet?" Mrs. Smoother asked curiously.

"Well, the doctor still wants me to take it easy, so I might work part-time at the community center for the summer. But that's all right now. I'm not sure what I want to do. Someday, I would love to have my own counseling clinic. I could do grief counseling, drug and alcohol counseling and different kinds of work such as groups counseling, and even youth counseling groups. I don't know what something like that would take to put together. I would need a lot of money, and I think I would have to get my doctorate or become a therapist, before I could do something like that, but it's just a dream," Angelina said as she shrugged her shoulders.

"That's a great idea. I could look into some things for you and find out how you could make that work. You know I would back you up in any way I can even if I have to be a partner. I will do that for you, if that is really something you want to do," Henry's said while taking a drink of his wine.

Henry was a therapist and he knows a lot about owning a business, because he had his own practice. Angelina was surprised he offered to help her, but he didn't offer her a job at his practice. She didn't want to work for Henry anyway. She loved him very much, but they were very different people, and he was very controlling about things.

"Angelina, that's a great idea. I would love to work in a place like that. We should really think about opening a counseling center up together. With Henry's help, we could do it, and I have a business degree," Harrison said, very enthusiastic.

Eva's face went white, and just before she could speak, Henry's dad spoke first, taking the words right out of her mouth, and he made them sound better. She was grateful he spoke first.

"That would be a big commitment—opening up a business together—it could ruin your relationship or the business altogether and the cost of something like that. It all would be really hard," Mr. Smoother said, trying to be helpful.

Harrison looked at Angelina with a smile on his face, and he held her hand. She shook her head. She wanted to wait, but he knew she was just nervous.

"Well, it's just a thought like Angelina said, just a dream, but sometimes dreams come true, and I think it could work out in the future," Harrison said. Angelina was relieved when the waitress came over and took everyone's orders.

"So, Angelina, you asked all of us here to talk about opening up your own business? Which I think it is a great idea, with the help of Henry. But was that what you wanted to talk about or was it about something else?" Father Patrick asked curiously. He knew something was up with her, but he could not figure out what it was.

Everyone's eyes were on Angelina. She was so nervous. She was shaking. Harrison was sitting beside her and could see how nervous she was.

"Well, we both wanted to talk to all of you. We want your love and support. The last few months have been really intense and have really made us evaluate what's important in our lives. We don't want to miss out on anything," he spoke. Everyone was listening so intently to Harrison.

But Eva and Angelina were looking directly at each other as if they both knew what was coming next. Everyone else was looking at Harrison, before he could finish what he was going to say, Angelina lifted up her left hand so everyone could see the big beautiful ring on her finger. She just continued looking at her aunt, waiting to get a response. But before Eva could do or say anything, Harrison's friend Matthew choked on his drink, spitting soda everywhere.

"Is that an engagement ring? Are you two getting married?" Matt said, with a disturbed look on his face.

"Yes, we are engaged, and we really want all of your support," Harrison said with hope in his voice. He was worried if things didn't go good tonight, Angelina would change her mind about them getting married.

No one said anything at first. Everyone was shocked. They all just sat there in silence for what seemed like hours to Angelina. The twins both started laughing and cheering; the kids were happy. Angelina and Eva just kept staring at each other. Angelina's hand was still up in the air, showing off the ring.

"Well, congratulations! That's a beautiful ring, and you two make a beautiful couple," Mrs. Smoother said in a happy voice. She could see tears building up in Angelina's eyes, and she didn't want her to be sad. An engagement was a happy occasion, but sitting at this table, you wouldn't think so.

"Thank you. We are really happy," Harrison said with relief in his voice that someone broke the silence.

"Yeah, man, congrats!" Matt said with hesitation in his voice.

Eva stood up and walked over to Angelina. She grabbed her hand, lifted her off her chair, and looked at Angelina's face. She had tears building up in her eyes, and she was shaking but still had the biggest smile on her face. Eva grabbed her and gave her a big hug. Angelina could feel herself relax, and her heartbeat slowed down. Then she stopped shaking. She held on to her aunt so tight. She was happy. That hug made her feel supported and loved.

"You know when it is right, and I know this is so right," Angelina whispered in her ear as they hugged.

Eva whispered back to her, "I love you. Congratulations!" Eva looked down at Harrison, who was watching them both with a concerned look on his face.

"You get in here, too. I love you both, and I'm happy for both of you." Eva smiled with her arms open, and she hugged them both.

Everyone sat back down. Henry's dad called the waitress over and got a bottle of wine brought to the table to celebrate. Henry poured the glasses and made the toast.

"Angelina and Harrison, congratulations! We all love and support you and wish you many happy years to come." Everyone cheered.

"Father Patrick, we would love for you to marry us at St. Mary's church, where my parents got married," Angelina said, looking at him with her big happy eyes.

Father Patrick stood up; he was getting emotional too. "Congrats! I would be honored to perform you wedding ceremony," he said with a warm, comforting voice. Angelina was so happy.

She went over and gave Father Patrick a big hug. The food came, and everyone ate and chatted about the wedding.

"Were you two considering next summer? Because the church fills up fast in the summer and most people book a year in advance, so you should come in and book your date soon," Father Patrick said as he was finishing his dinner.

"Well, actually, we were thinking about fall, like November," Angelina said, and everyone shook their heads in agreement.

"Yeah that will be nice and give you lots of time."

"No, we were thinking like this fall, as in like five months from now," she said with a funny look on her face, just waiting to see everyone's reactions.

"Why so fast? Are you pregnant?" Matt blurted out. Everyone's face was in shock, waiting for her answer.

"No it's not even like that." She got a little mad.

"We just want to be married, and I just want to do it fast. I don't need a big fancy wedding, so we don't need a long engagement. Eva and Henry were only together for nine months before they got married and knew each other only for five months before they got engaged. We have known each other for over five years and have been good friends for the last three. I died, and after something like that happens, you want to do everything so you don't miss out on life. You can accomplish so much in your life, but if you don't have someone to share it with, then you're all alone." Angelina was crying she wasn't sad just emotional Harrison held her hand for support.

"You are right, Angelina, I get what you are saying, and we support you," Henry said, shaking his head like he really did understand.

After dinner, everyone hugged and said there good-byes. Harrison and Angelina went back to her place. Later that night, they were lying in the bed, talking:

"How do you feel tonight went? Are you happy with everything?" he asked.

"Yes, I am happy. I think that everyone supports us even if they think it's too fast. I know it's fast, but I don't care, because I am so happy and so in love with you." As Angelina climbed on top of him and started kissing him, Harrison didn't have a chance to say anything else.

CHAPTER 14

The summer was going so fast. Harrison got a job at a center for drug addictions. It was only twenty-five hours a week in the evening, but he was just happy to be working in his field and getting experience.

Angelina was working part-time, too, for Dr. Dina Hayford in her clinic. She hired her to do grief counseling. Angelina was really enjoyed helping the people she worked with. She was also working at the community center but only one day a week. Angelina was mainly helping the clients deal with the loss of a loved one. But one Wednesday, Dina gave her the Clinton family to work with.

The father was terminally ill with cancer, and he only had a few months left according to his doctors. He was married and had two daughters—thirteen and fifteen years old. He wanted them all to get counseling together. Angelina was nervous. She was afraid of saying the wrong thing or pushing too much. She was confused. *How do you do grief counseling when the person is still alive?* The family all sat on chairs, looking at each other.

"I am going to be honest. I have never done a group session like this before, but I am here to help. So I think we should start by having each one of you talk first, by saying one thing that's bugging you the most. Then we can go from there," Angelina spoke, trying to be calm and maintain professionalism.

Angelina was nervous, but she could see the fear and pain in the family members' eyes, and she wanted to help them while they still had time together.

The youngest girl, Amber, talked first. "I am sad because I don't want my dad to die. I don't want our lives to be changed. I am sad because it had changed so much already. He is still here, and we are all sad all the time, and it sucks," she said in a very squeaky voice, and then she began to cry.

Then the older daughter, Amy, spoke. "I feel so helpless. I can't do anything to change the fact that my dad is going to die. I am sad all the time, every moment of every day, and our time together is bitter sweet. It hurts to know we don't have much time, and it hurts to be together, too," she said, choking back her tears, like she had to be strong, as she looked at her little sister and held her hand.

Then the mother spoke. "I am so lost. The thought of my partner in life not being here with me anymore terrifies me. He is my other half. I am not whole without him. How do I go on with my life without him? And I don't know how to support him now. We are all so scared. I feel like I don't know how to deal with my own feelings, let alone support my husband and my girls," she spoke with so much love in her voice. She was heartbroken, and he wasn't even gone yet.

Then Mr. Clinton spoke. "I am scared to die. I am afraid of what happens next. I am scared for my family. How will they deal with losing me? And I am sad to say good-bye. It kills me to know that I won't be there on the most important days of their lives. I won't get to see them graduate or get married or see my grandchildren. I feel like I am letting them down, like I am not strong enough to fight this cancer," he spoke in a very deep, strong voice with no hesitation. But she could hear the pain in his voice and see the pain that was there in his eyes. The whole family was crying and trying not to look at each other.

"Everything that all of you are feeling is perfectly normal. Did you notice something every one of you said?" she asked, looking at all of them.

They all looked at each other, confused. They couldn't make a connection.

"Every one of you is scared and sad. You are all feeling the same things in different ways. What you are all going through is very hard, and no one knows how to deal with dying or death. All I can say is life is going to change. It is going to be hard, and there are times when you will feel like you don't know how you can do this, but you will. You all have something very special that not everyone gets." Angelina took a breath. She was trying to stay professional and not get emotionally involved, but she didn't know how to do that.

"You all know it's coming, so you have *time*. Time to be together, time to tell each other everything you want the other person to know. You all have each other to lean on. Don't hold back, don't try to be strong, be honest. Be there. Love each other, do things as a family, or maybe make time to do things just one-on-one. Often people say to me that they feel the worst because they didn't get a chance to say good-bye or they regretted not telling the person something. You four don't have to have any regrets. You can tell each other everything you want to say. As bad as things feel right now, you all have something very special—time. And you have each other," Angelina spoke with intense passion. She envied what they had—time and knowledge.

The family talked with Angelina for an hour. At the end of the session, Amy came up to Angelina. She had tears running down her face. "Thank you for reminding us of what's important. You are right. We get to say good-bye, and that's a good thing, so thanks." She hugged Angelina and then left with her family.

Angelina was starting to build a good friendship with Dina. They had lunch together on days when she worked. Things were going good, and the wedding plans were moving along nicely. Almost everything was set; the ceremony would be at St. Mary's church on Saturday, November 25, one month before Christmas at 4:00 p.m. Dinner and reception to follow at Antonio's Italian restaurant. They rented out the upstairs hall for parties. It's beautifully decorated, but it's not very big, which was perfect for their wedding. The restaurant supplied everything they would need for the reception. The big things were planned for the wedding, but Angelina still didn't have a wedding dress. So Eva and Angelina planned a day to go out and find a dress, look for flowers and look at wedding cakes. Angelina and Eva walked into a bridal store. Angelina was overwhelmed; she had never been one for shopping.

"Do you, ladies, need help finding something?" Tiffany the sales girl, asked pleasantly.

"Yes, we are looking for a wedding dress for my niece," Eva said, putting her arm around Angelina and smiling.

"She is getting married in three months, so we need something that can be ordered quickly or off the rack."

Tiffany looked at Angelina and spun her around, checking her out. "So do you know what you want? If you give me some ideas, then I will pull some gowns out for you and you can try them on."

Angelina felt so uncomfortable about people paying so much attention to her. It was weird, but she did know what she wanted. "Yes, I want something ivory or an off-white, all lace, very simple, nothing big or puffy, comfortable not heavy, straps or strapless, something that shows off my shape, and it could be short or long." Angelina was feeling excited. This was real; she was in a wedding dress shop.

"OK, well it sounds like you know what you want, I will pick out a few dresses for you and I'll be right back," Tiffany said. She was very bubbly.

Angelina and Eva both sat down on a black couch and chatted

until the sales girl came back with some dresses for Angelina to try on.

"I am so excited to be here with you, trying on wedding dresses," Eva said, clapping her hands with excitement. "I can't believe you are marrying my nephew," she said, making a funny face. "But you two are so cute together. I love it. It was weird at first, but I can see how good you are for each other."

"I am so happy that you are here with me, too, and I wanted to talk to you. Harrison is having his friend Matt as his best man, and I would like for you to be my maid of honor. I was hoping that Henry would give me away and that the twins could be in the wedding, too." Eva was emotional but happy at the same time. She was honored to be in the wedding. She was very excited.

"Yes, we would love to be a part of the wedding, and I will have to find a dress and pick out cute outfits for the twins. What color dress do you want me to wear?" Eva asked excitedly.

"You don't have to go out and buy a new dress. You can wear whatever you want to. I would like it to be blue, but it doesn't have to be. We decided blue because my ring is a blue sapphire. So we just made that as our wedding color," Angelina smiled as she looked at her ring all proud of how beautiful it was.

"Give me any reason to buy a new dress! Of course, I will buy one for your wedding, silly girl. Shopping is fun," Eva said, laughing.

Tiffany came back with her arms full of dresses and lead Angelina into a dressing room. The first dress she tried on was an ivory lace dress with cap sleeves and a sweetheart neckline, very fitted to the body and flew out after the hips.

When she walked out of the dressing room, her aunt was standing beside two other ladies that worked in the store. They all looked at her. She looked so beautiful in the dress.

Angelina stepped out and looked in the mirror and saw herself for the first time in a wedding dress. She looked like a bride. The dress was beautiful and she looked stunning, but she looked at the price tag, and it was $2,500. She knew her aunt or Harrison would buy it for her. But she wasn't the type of girl that needed to spend that much money on a dress, not when there were people in the world that didn't have food.

"Wow, Angelina, you look amazing! Do you like this one?" Eva asked.

"Yes, I do. I think I look really pretty in it, and it's a beautiful dress, but I would like to try on a few more before I make a decision," Angelina said, but she was a little disappointed because it was the dress she wanted. She wished she hadn't even tried it on, because it was perfect, and Angelina was worried she wouldn't find something that would compare to how beautiful it was. She tried on another dress; the second dress was simple, strapless, A-line dress, but it was really white and only had lace on the bottom of the dress.

"This is nice, but the other one was better," Eva said.

"Yes, I don't like this one as much either, but I still have a couple more to try on." Angelina responded.

Angelina went back into the changing room, feeling a little down, hoping that she could find a dress she loved as much as the first one. Tiffany had a dress in her hands.

"This dress is on sale, and it's off the rack, so you would have to take it as it is, and if it doesn't fit you perfectly, then you would have to get that fixed by yourself. But I think you might like this one, it has an old fashion feel to it, and it is simple but classic," Tiffany said, smiling really confident about the dress.

Angelina put on the third dress and came out of the dressing room. Everyone stopped talking and just looked at her. She hadn't seen herself the mirror yet, but it was comfortable and fitted her really nice.

"It's perfect for you," Eva said smiling with tears in her eyes.

Angelina stood in front of the mirror and looked at herself in this dress. The dress was perfect for her. It was similar to the first dress. It was an off-white lace dress with a cap sleeve but had a square neckline. It fitted to the hip and then flowed out, but it was short, it went only to the calf in the front, and then in the back, it went longer like a short train. It was simple but classic, and it had a dark blue sash around the waist.

"It is perfect for me. It even has the right colored sash." Angelina smiled. Her face lit up with joy. She looked like an Angel. She felt beautiful, which was something she had never really felt before.

Tiffany came over with some accessories to finish off the

wedding look. She brought out a couple of pairs of shoes. One pair was dark blue in color. Angelina loved the blue peekaboo shoes. Tiffany also brought out a very simple headband that had clear crystals and blue crystals on it. She placed it on Angelina's head and put a simple veil with lace, just on the bottom edge. Angelina stood up on a pedestal; she had on the perfect dress with blue shoes and the blue headband with the veil, and Eva had the biggest smile on her face and tears in her eyes.

"Wow, Angelina, do you ever look like your mother. You are so beautiful," Eva said, wiping her tears away. "How do you feel? Is this the dress?"

"This is the dress that I am going to wear, when I get married. I feel radiant in this dress." She had tears running down her cheeks and the biggest smile on her face. She was glowing with happiness. "I just wish my parents were here."

Eva gave her a hug, and they both had an emotional moment. "This is the dress we want. How much is it anyway?" Eva asked

"This dress is off the rack. It's a take it as is, but it's on sale for $500," she said, smiling.

"Wow! That is amazing. It really is the perfect dress," Angelina said with relief because it was inexpensive.

"Henry and I have decided to buy your wedding dress and accessories. As your acting parents, that's what we want to do. So do you want the blue shoes and the headband and the veil, too?" Eva asked.

"Thank you. That is very nice, but this is all too much," Angelina said, feeling overwhelmed by the gesture.

"Honey, I thought the dress alone was going to be over $2,000. So it's really not too much. This is what we want to do for you," Eva said laughing; like spending $700 on her was no big deal.

After they were done and paid for all Angelina's stuff, Eva found the perfect dress for her, and it was also blue and on sale too. They walked over to a little bakery to look for wedding cakes. They got to sample a few. The man at the bakery gave Angelina a booklet to take home and look at. Then they went to look at flowers. She picked out white lilies for the wedding they were sweet and simple.

On their way home, they chatted about things. "So have you guys decided where you want to live once you're married?" Eva asked.

Angelina made a mad face and shook her head. "Well, we have been arguing about it, because he wants to buy a house. And I want to stay in the building. I think we could live in my apartment until something bigger opens up, but he wants to buy a big fancy house," Angelina said, annoyed.

"Well, I can understand him not wanting to live in your apartment. There would be no room for any of his stuff and it would feel like it was just your place. I can understand him wanting to have a place that belongs to both of you. You want to wait for a bigger apartment to open up, it could be years before that happens," Eva said looking at her. "I don't want you to move, but maybe it's not a bad idea. Maybe, you could find something close by so we can still see each other all the time."

"Well, I guess you are right. Maybe, I should at least look at places and be more open minded. Maybe, I will feel better after looking. It's just that so much is changing. It's a lot. I am excited but nervous too. Thank you, Aunt Eva, for today. It was fun doing wedding stuff with you." Angelina asked.

"I had fun, too. I'm going to keep your wedding dress at my place until the wedding, so it is safe from anyone seeing it," she said as they were walking into their building.

Angelina walked into her apartment, and it smelt so good; food was being cooked, and the dining room table was set with candles and flowers. Harrison walked out of the kitchen with a very big smile on his face. "Great! You are home. I made you dinner—homemade spaghetti. Have a seat, I'll be there in just a few more minutes," he said with a nervous giggle.

Angelina sat down at the table. Harrison came from behind her and kissed her neck and wrapped his arms around her body, holding her really tight. "How was your day with Eva? Did you find your dress?" he asked.

"Thank you for making dinner. I didn't think you would be here. I thought you had to work tonight." She said as she turned around and touched his face and kissed his lips.

"I was supposed to work tonight, but I got called into work a day shift. So now I get to spend the evening with you," he said as he kissed her nose.

"Well, good I am glad you are home."

"You didn't answer me, did you find a dress?" he asked all excited.

"Well, we had a really nice day, and I found the perfect dress, and Aunt Eva bought it for me as a gift." She smiled. He could see she was so happy and that made him feel good.

"The prices of the wedding dresses are crazy. Did you know that? They are like $2,000. That is crazy. I didn't know that." She laughed, shaking her head.

"Yes, I know that wedding dresses were very expensive, but I bet you found the cheapest dress in the whole store," he said with a smile looking at her.

"Well, maybe I did. But the truth is I fell in love with the dress before I knew the price," she said, giggling. She was so excited she felt like a kid at Christmas. Angelina could tell something was up. He was acting funny. He was very hyper.

"Hey, why are you being so sweet? I thought you are mad at me, for not wanting to move?" she said looking at him, and he made a funny face.

"Well, you may become mad at me now, because I did something bad today," he said with a mischievous look on his face.

Angelina was nervous. This was it! She had been waiting for months for something to go wrong. Nothing good ever lasted in her life. She was shaking, and her heart was beating so fast.

"Tell me, what's wrong? You have changed your mind, right? You don't love me anymore." The words escaped from her lips. She didn't even have a chance to think. She just spoke. She was crying on the inside, her body ached while she waited to hear his response.

"What? No." He wrapped his arms around her. "I love you. That's never going to change. But you might just be a little mad at me," he said.

"Why? What did you do?" she asked curiously. Now that she knew he was not breaking up with her, she wasn't that worried.

"I found the perfect house for us on the internet, and I called the real estate agent. I went to see the house after work today, and it really is perfect. I think you would love it, and I am hoping you will come and look at it with me tomorrow." Harrison said. Angelina didn't say anything for a minute. She got up and went to the bathroom, came back, sat down, and looked at him.

"I didn't want to move because I am scared," she said, not making eye contact with him. She was mad at him.

"I am hurt. You thought that it would be a good idea to go look at a house without me. Well, I feel that was unfair. You didn't even give me a chance to get used to the idea of moving. I had been thinking about moving, because this place will always feel like just mine, and we should have a place that is ours. I was going to tell you tonight that we could go look at places together, but you just went and did it on your own," she said. He could hear the hurt in her voice, and her face told him that she was disappointed.

"I am sorry. You are right, it was unfair of me to do that without you," he said, his eyes looked sad. "We should have talked about it more, and I shouldn't have gone without you, but seriously, the house is so nice. I really do think you will like it. Will you come see it with me tomorrow morning, before you go to work? Please?" Harrison pleaded.

"Yes, I will go with you to look at the house, but I am still mad at you," she said, pouting.

"I am sorry," he said, hugging her. "Are you hungry? Dinner is ready."

"Yes, I am really hungry," Angelina replied.

"You just sit and relax. I will make you a plate," he said, walking into the kitchen.

He came back out a few minutes later with a plate of spaghetti and a glass of wine for her, and then he went and got his plate, and they ate together.

"Dinner was fantastic. Thank you very much," she said as they were washing the dishes.

"I know you are mad at me. Can I make it up by taking you out to a movie?" Harrison asked.

"OK, I would like to go to a movie. Do you know what's playing?" said Angelina.

"No, I'm not sure. Let's just go and pick a movie once we get there." Harrison replied.

"OK, I'll get cleaned up, then we can go," Angelina said with a smile on her face.

CHAPTER 15

The next day, they got dressed and went to meet with the real estate agent, to go and look at the house. They walked out of their building and met Jane, the real estate agent who was waiting outside. Angelina was confused as to why they were meeting there. *Shouldn't they meet her at the house?*

"Hello, Jane, it is nice to see you again. This is my fiancée, Angelina." Harrison said.

Angelina shook her hand. She really liked being introduced as his fiancée. It made her giggle a little.

"Hello, nice to meet you, Angelina. This is a great area to live, but you already know that. Well, shall we go?" asked Jane.

"Where is the house?" Angelina asked, looking around confused.

Jane pointed across the street to a row of beautiful Victorian town houses. Angelina had dreamed of living in one of those houses since she was a little girl. The houses were beautiful and were so close to Aunt Eva's. Angelina grabbed Harrison's arm. She was so excited but also nervous.

"How can we afford for a place like this? It has to be like a million dollars," exclaimed Angelina.

"It's fine. Don't worry, we can afford it. Remember? I told you I have a lot of money. It's fine. Let's just see if you like the house first," he said, holding her hand as they crossed the street.

Of course, she was going to like the house. It was perfect, and she hadn't even stepped inside the front door, and she was already in love with the house. There were about five houses in a row. The house for sale was the last house on the corner. The house was really big, all gray brick. It was old but had a modern feel to it. It had so much character—white shutters, a big porch, and big bay windows on both sides of the door. It was so nice. They walked into the entrance way, It had a closet to hang jackets and put shoes, and had marble tiles on the floor.

"The house has hardwood floors throughout, but there are marble tiles in kitchen and the bathrooms," Jane said.

Right off the mudroom was a formal living room; it was of good size with lots of natural light coming in from the big bay window. It was a living/dining room combination all open concept. The walls were of a dark blue color. There was white trim and crown molding on the ceilings. A big beautiful white fireplace was in the room, which made it cozy. The formal dining room was connected to the living room by just an archway, dividing up the space. The dining room was also of a good size. The walls were of a soft gray; one wall had strips painted on it. The room was very nice and had a big table and chairs. Then they walked into the kitchen. It was huge. It had dark wooden cabinets with brown and beige granite countertops. A big fancy island was located in the middle of the kitchen where the sink was and it had big stainless steel appliances. Right off the kitchen was a sunken family room. The walls were of a taupe color. The room had a sliding glass door leading to a back deck. Then they went upstairs. There was an open office space with white shelves built onto the walls.

"This area would be perfect for all your books. It would be like your own library." Harrison smiled at Angelina, really trying to sell her on the house.

There were three good sized bedrooms on that level, with a bathroom. They went up another level.

"I call this level, the lover's suite, or master wing," Jane said as they climbed the stairs.

A suite it was. The master bedroom was huge. The walls were of soft brown color, and one accent wall was dark red. The room had a king size bed in it, with four-piece dresser set. There were two chairs and a fireplace, off the bedroom was a huge walk-in closet and a bathroom that had a stand up glassed-in shower with a chair and a corner Jacuzzi tub, big enough for two and it had his and her sinks and mirrors.

After that, they went back downstairs, Harrison was so

excited. "Now my favorite part," he said with a happy look on his face.

"This house is amazing, but is there more?" Angelina said in a way that made the house sound too big, more space than the two of them needed.

"Yes there is a basement apartment, which you could rent out or turn into a business space. The people that own it now rented it out, but before that, it was used as a dentist office," Jane said.

Jane showed Angelina and Harrison the basement next. It was a cute apartment. Everything was baggie, and the floors were of hardwood. The living room was of a good size, and the kitchen was small. It was just off the living room. The two bedrooms were both small but had closets, and it had a cute bathroom.

"I know I am jumping the gun, but think, Angelina, this could be perfect for our own business. We could have a counseling center in this space. It would be perfect if we could do group counseling in the common area and private sessions in the rooms," Harrison said.

"You think of everything. This house is amazing, but can we afford this place? How much is it?" Angelina asked. Jane handed Angelina a copy of the listing. Angelina blinked twice.

"This house is actually listed under market value right now, because the owner wants it gone fast, but I'll let you two talk the house, and I'll be upstairs," Jane said.

"I love this house. I think it's perfect, and the location is perfect, too. We could have a future here. We could rent this part out for a while, and maybe, in the future, turn it into a business. This is perfect. Do you like it? I want to make an offer, and please don't think about the money. If that doesn't matter, would you want to live in this house?" Harrison asked her, touching her hands and looking into his eyes.

"Yes, I love this house. It's perfect, I agree with you. But if we are partners you have to fill me in on how we can afford this place. It's over a million dollars," exclaimed Angelina.

"My parents' house was over two when I sold it. I put all the money in the bank and moved in to the apartment. At that time, in my life, I didn't care about having nice things, but now I have you. My plan is to buy the house out, no mortgage. I have more than enough money to buy this house and still have lots left over," said Harrison.

"We can rent out the basement apartment as well. That would cover all our bills. We could continue working part-time and gain experience. If you wanted to go back to school to become a psychiatrist you could. I really want this house. It is a good investment, and there will always be value here. So if we sell someday, we could make money from this place. All you have to do is to say yes." Harrison was holding Angelina in his arms and had the biggest smile on his face.

"OK, if I agree, then you have to let me put in some money, too. I have about $20K left over from my parents' life insurance. I can't let you pay for everything. This house has to be both of ours," Angelina said, smiling.

"Yes, that's fare. I can do that," Harrison said, laughing with excitement.

"Then yes, I want to buy this house with you and start our future here together," she smiled and then she made a funny face. "I am a little intimidated about having to clean it, this house is huge," They both laughed.

"I love you so much, I can't wait." His eyes lit up with excitement, and he kissed her like five time he was so happy.

They went upstairs to talk to Jane and put in an offer. Jane to assured then she would get back to them as soon as she possibly could. That night, Harrison had to work the evening shift again, so Angelina had dinner with Eva and the family.

"So what's new, Angelina?" Henry asked while eating his dinner.

"Well, I am glad you asked. Harrison and I have decided to buy a place of our own," Angelina said, smiling and giggling with joy.

"Yes, well, your aunt mentioned something about that." Henry replied.

"That's good. Are you two going to wait until after the wedding?" Eva asked.

"Well, we went to look at a town house yesterday, and we put an offer on it. We are really excited. Jane, our real estate agent told us we would hear back tomorrow," Angelina said, smiling while she took another bite of her dinner.

"Wow! You two move so fast." The words just escaped from Henry's mouth, he then looked up at Angelina, hoping he didn't offend her. "I am sorry. I didn't mean that in a bad way."

"No, it's OK. I understand. We are moving fast, but if I die tomorrow, I won't have any regrets. Next time, I won't need to come back," she said while taking a drink and looked him straight in the eyes with a big smile on her face.

"Well, I think you should wait until after the wedding to move in together, but I am happy for you and with whatever you have decided," Eva said with a funny smile on her face. Her words didn't match her expression at all.

"So where is the place you two looked at?" Henry asked while taking a bite of his steak.

"Hmm . . . across the street. The Victorian town house on the corner. That's for sale," she said embarrassed.

Henry started to cough; he almost choked. He took a drink and then cleared his throat. "What? Really? You two can afford a place like that?" he asked, shaking his head in shock. "Why haven't we been charging them more for rent?" he said, laughing and looking at Eva.

"Yeah, well, Harrison has it all worked out. We are using our inheritances from our parents," she said, looking down at her almost empty plate.

"Well, good for you both," Eva said, looking at Henry and making a funny face.

"So are you still OK to watch the kids tonight?" Henry asked.

"Yes, of course, we have lots of plans. We are going to make a fort. We have it all planned out and it should be fun," Angelina said, smiling at the twins, and they both started to laugh.

After dinner, Angelina watched the twins so Eva and Henry could go out to a movie. Harrison was asleep on the couch when Angelina came home. She woke him up, and they went to bed.

The next morning, while they were having breakfast, Jane called to tell them that the offer was accepted with conditions.

"The house is ours, but the condition is we take over in four weeks," Harrison said.

Angelina felt stressed and anxious. She started to breath really heavy, and her palms got sweaty. "Can we do that? We have so much going on right now," she said, looking at him with worry in her big brown eyes. "So we would move in September, go away in October with the family, and then we're getting married in November," she said looking at him. "Can we make this work?"

"Yes, we can do this. It's going to be crazy busy, but we can make it work," Harrison said, looking at her with a hopeful look on his face.

"We have to meet with Jane, sign the papers, and then get to the bank and move some money around." Harrison said.

"OK. So, we are really going to do this," Angelina said. Harrison flashed his big beautiful smile.

The house was inspected and everything went through; it was official, they had purchased their first house. They took Eva and Harrison over to see the house before they moved. Everyone loved the house. The next few weeks were really busy. They had to go through both of their apartments and decide what to keep and what to give away. They went out and bought some new furniture for their very large house, which was perfect because it would delivered and set up for them the week they were to move in.

Time was flying by and before they knew it, it was time to move into their new home. Henry and Eva, Harrison's friend, Matthew, and his girlfriend, Gwen, helped them move.

"You two have a really nice two-bedroom apartment downstairs. Are going to rent it out?" Matt asked with an interested look on his face.

"Yes, we are going to rent it out at some point and then eventually turn it into a counseling clinic," Harrison said, not picking up on Matt's hints.

"Why? Do you know anyone looking for a place?" Angelina asked, smiling. She knew he wanted the apartment.

"Well, Gwen and I are looking for a place. I don't know if it would be weird, but we would love to have the apartment. It is really nice." Matt replied.

"That would be OK with me, I would rather have someone we know as tenants than strangers," Angelina said looking over at Harrison.

"How much would you charge for rent?" Gwen asked with a worried look on her face.

"We really haven't thought about it. Things have been happening so fast. What could you afford?" Harrison asked. "We don't even know what an apartment like that would go for."

"Well, we are hoping to find something in between $1,100 and $1,300. That's really all we could afford, but finding a decent place in Toronto is really hard," Gwen said.

Harrison looked at Angelina for the OK, and she smiled and shook her head.

"The apartment is yours. If you two want it, you can have it for $900 a month, all inclusive," Harrison said.

"Really? You know you could get a lot more for an apartment like that," Matt said. "But that would be so great. We were hoping to find something for November would that be OK with you two, if that's when we move in?"

"That would be great because that will give us some time alone and time to get the place organized," Angelina said as she began to unpack a box.

Henry ordered in pizza for lunch. Eva and Henry stayed and helped them unpack and organize things, and then they went home to relax. Henry and Harrison spent all afternoon upstairs. They got the bedroom all set up so they had a place to sleep that night. Once everyone was gone, Angelina went up to see what Harrison had accomplished in their bedroom.

Harrison was in the bathroom, running the bathtub when she came in, he had candles and music going. He looked up and saw her standing there, watching him.

"You caught me. I was trying to be romantic and run you a nice and relaxing bath." Angelina grabbed Harrison and kissed him.

"You are too cute, and this was very romantic of you," she said, smiling as she was starting to undress, trying to be sexy and seductive. Then she looked at herself in the mirror, and she saw the scar on her stomach. She put her hands over it to cover it up. She didn't breathe for a minute; it was like, in that moment, she relived getting shot all over again. She couldn't breathe; tears were starting to build up in her eyes. She never thought she looked good before, but she didn't look like she did now; her stomach had marks that went in all different directions from the stitches. It was healing, but it looked horrible. In her mind she looked like a monster. Why would anyone want to be with someone who looked like that? She cried and tried to hide herself away from him.

Harrison pulled her hand off her stomach and looked into her big brown eyes that looked so sad. "You are so beautiful!" he said as he pulled her close to him. He put his hands on her face and gently pressed his lips on hers; it was a sweet, intimate kiss.

"I never thought I would love someone this much. Everything about you is amazing," he spoke, and she tried to move away and cover her stomach up. She was making a sad face. He pulled her back to him. "This scar makes you even more beautiful, because it takes a really amazing person to save someone's life. You have this scar because you are a beautiful person, and I love everything about you and your body," he said, smiling.

Angelina was overjoyed by how his words made her feel so loved and so special. She started kissing him and taking his clothes off.

"I drew you a bath so you could relax. I wanted you to enjoy yourself. You worked hard today."

She smiled at him, holding his hand as she finished undressing and got into the bathtub.

"This tub is big enough for two, come relax with me," she said, her big eyes glowing with love and happiness. "You worked far harder than I did today. No one let me lift anything."

"Because we love you, and we don't want you to get hurt," Harrison replied.

He got into the tub with her, and she laid there in his arms. Everything, for the first time in their lives, felt perfect.

CHAPTER 16

After a few weeks, Angelina and Harrison had the house all organized. The wedding plans were all coming together. Eva had planned a house warming/birthday/engagement party for Angelina and Harrison on September 20, at their new house. Friends and family came to celebrate with them. The house was full of people. Everyone seemed to be having a good time. But Harrison was worried about Angelina. He could tell something was wrong with her. She had been acting funny all day; she was clumsy and not making sense when she spoke. She was walking around, but she looked lost and confused like she didn't understand what was going on.

She was as white as a ghost and shaking. She had a smile on her face, and she was being friendly to people, but something was wrong. Angelina went into the kitchen to get a drink, and Harrison followed her.

"Angelina, what is wrong? Harrison asked. "You don't look well, and you are shaking."

Angelina just stood there and looked at him with this lost-and-confused expression on her face and tears in her eyes.

"I feel things and sense things, and I am scared. I feel really sad, and I have a bad feeling. Something really bad is going to happen, but I don't know what or why I feel this way. But it's going to happen soon—something to someone I love. Please, don't think that I'm crazy," she said in a hoarse voice. Harrison gave her a hug. He was really worried about her.

"I don't think you're crazy. Sometimes, people get that feeling. Maybe it's not as bad as you think it's going to be," he said, trying to make her feel better.

Angelina took a deep breath, and tried to shake her bad feeling, and they went back into the living room. When Father Patrick showed up, Angelina was drawn to him. She didn't leave his side. She talked to him most at the party. He looked different to her, like his skin was shimmering, and then, when she gave him a hug, she felt something special. She knew in her heart that Father Patrick was going to go to heaven soon. She was the only person who saw him differently. She took Father Patrick on a private tour of the house so she could talk to him.

"So, Father Patrick, how are you feeling these days?" she asked him. She was worried about him.

"Well, for an old man, I am doing well. I am feeling really good today, like I have more energy than I have had in years, and I just feel so happy, like something really good is coming. I know it's funny, but that's just how I feel," he replied, Angelina was holding back her tears. She took comfort in knowing that he was feeling good.

"I just wanted to ask you a weird question. Ever since the day I died, I have felt different, like more alive in some way. Now that I have had that experience, I am not scared to die, because I know someday I get to go to heaven. I was wondering are you afraid to die?" she asked, looking at him so intensely. She was so sad that she felt this way.

"No I am not afraid to die. I am an old man, and I have lived a long life doing God's work, and I hope he is proud of me. I have helped a lot of people in my days, and I have seen many things. I have good friends and family and I know where I am going. It is going to be perfect. I don't want to die, but when it's my time to go, I know it will be, because God is calling me home," he said smiling, and she smiled at him.

"It is perfect there. I only saw a glimpse, but it was amazing, and the love I felt will stay with me always. I love you, Father Patrick. You have always been there for me for my whole life. I have always been able to count on you, no matter what, and I just wanted to say thank you, and if you ever need me, I am here for you, too." She gave him a big hug and held on to him for a long time.

"I am so happy that I have been able to be here for you, my child. I also love you, and I am proud of the woman you have become. Your parents would be proud, too. I can't wait for your wedding. I think Harrison is really a good man, and you two make good partners. You can count on him. I can see how much you two love each other," he said, looking into her eyes. She wanted to tell him, but she felt in a way that he already knew. She wanted to cry and to scream and to pray to God not to take him, but she couldn't, because she knew it was his time.

She finished showing Father Patrick the house, and then they went back to the party, after they talked. She knew that when it was his time to go, he would be in good hands.

"You look like you are feeling better," Harrison said, walking over to her with a glass of wine. He then handed it to her and kissed her. He was relieved that she was smiling and looking better.

"Yes, I am. I just needed to talk to Father Patrick," she said. She wasn't keeping it from him but she didn't want to worry him more.

Then Eva came out with a big cake, and everyone sang happy birthday, and they blew out their candles, and Angelina made a wish she knew would come true. *I wish Father Patrick gets his wings, because he is already an Angel.*

Later that night, after the party was over and they finished cleaning up, Angelina couldn't sleep. She kept tossing and turning.

"I know something is bugging you. Maybe it would help if you talked to me, you are keeping me up anyway," Harrison said rolling over to look at her as they lay there on the bed.

"I want to tell you something, but I don't want you to think different of me. Ever since I woke up, I have felt different. I think I even look different. I haven't been able to place it until today. I think I have a special gift, and I am really scared. I think Father Patrick is going to die," she said while they were lying there in the bed. "I feel like it's going to be soon. I had a bad feeling all day, and then, when he walked in tonight, I saw him in a different way. He looked like he was shimmering like an Angel. I could be wrong, but the feeling is so strong," she said looking into his eyes, which looked so sad. She was worried that he was going to leave her because she was crazy.

Harrison didn't say anything. He just held her in his arms so tight that she could feel his heartbeat on her face. The phone rang, and Harrison looked at her with a scared expression on his face. Then he answered the phone, "Oh my god, we are on our way." He got off the bed and just looked at Angelina. "They just took Father Patrick to the hospital. They found him unconscious in his room."

When they got to the hospital, Eva was crying. She ran up to Angelina and gave her a big hug. "We are just waiting to hear what's going on. We don't know anything yet," Eva said to both, Angelina and Harrison.

Angelina just walked around the hospital. She already knew that Father Patrick had gone to heaven. She had feelings of sadness and a sense of peace. Angelina walked around the hospital on her own, she walked into a games room, where an old man was sitting all alone. When she looked at him, he was shimmering, and she got that feeling again.

She sat down beside the old man. He was wearing a pair of blue pajamas with matching slippers. He had thick white hair, a mustache, and little beady eyes. She couldn't even make out the color of them. He was hooked up to a few different machines that had wheels on them so he could move around.

"Hello, how are you?" Angelina asked.

"Are you here for me? No one ever comes to see me anymore. I am Jake, nice to meet you." The old man replied.

"Hello, Jake, I am Angelina. I saw you sitting all alone, and I thought maybe you could use a friend to talk to." Angelina responded.

"You are a nice girl, talking to an old man, I am lonely. I miss my wife. She died. We were together for fifty-three years. Now I am hopelessly waiting till I get to see her again. We had no kids, and everyone I knew is gone. So I am all alone left on this earth." She held his hand.

"Not tonight. You have me. I am your friend now. How are you feeling today?" Angelina asked.

"It's funny you ask me that. I am very sick. Every day I have pain, but not today, no pain. I feel good, and now I feel better that I am not all alone. I am not scared to die," he spoke with a strong British accent. "I just hate this part—the being alone and missing everyone—I wonder what happens next?"

Angelina told the man her story about how she died and what

it was all like for her. The man looked at her with big happy eyes. He saw her, and she was shimmering.

"You're here to guide me home, you are, my Angel?" he said.

Then Harrison walked into the games room. Angelina gave the man a hug and said good-bye.

"Thank you for sharing your story with me. It was nice to have a friend," he said with a funny grin, like he was telling a joke.

"Good–bye, my friend, enjoy your next journey." Angelina said.

Angelina walked out into the hallway, and Harrison was crying. She hugged him and tried to comfort him.

"It's OK, you can cry. I understand how hard this is," she said like she already knew what he was going to say next.

"Angelina, Father Patrick passed away, there was nothing they could do for him. I am so sorry." She fell into his arms and cried, even though she already knew it, hearing the words made it all more real.

As they were standing in the hallway, they heard beeps, and nurses ran into the room where the old man Jake was all alone. He died. They stood there in the hallway while they brought his body out. Angelina was so scared. She was shaking and crying. She looked at Harrison with a terrified shocked expression on her face.

"I knew he was going to die. Why? How did I know that two people were going to die today? She was crying and talking so fast.

Eva found her in the hallway and just held her for a long time. Angelina became hysterical and started screaming and crying. She couldn't control herself. A doctor examined her and gave her something to calm her down. He told her family that she was just in shock.

They took her home and put her in bed. Angelina had dreams. She was screaming and shaking all night. When she woke up in the morning, Harrison was lying beside her.

"Hi, how are you feeling?" he asked as he gave her a hug and kissed her cheek.

"I have a purpose on earth as I will in heaven," she spoke as if she wasn't really there. Her eyes hazed over, and the expression on her face terrified him. Then she fell back to sleep. She slept for days. Harrison was so worried about her that he had a doctor come and check her out.

When Angelina woke up, the doctor told her, she had post-traumatic stress disorder.

Angelina got out of bed, showered, got dressed, and went downstairs. Everyone she knew was at her house. When she walked into the kitchen, everyone looked at her like she was a ghost.

"How are you feeling?" Eva asked like she had been crying for days.

"I am OK. I am sorry for losing it there, but I am feeling a little better now. What is going on? Why is everyone here and all dressed up?" she asked, confused as she looked around at her friends and family. They all seemed frozen looking at her.

"Father Patrick's funeral is today. We are all going, but we feel you should stay here and relax. This might be too much for you to handle right now. You have been through so much," Eva spoke with fear. She didn't want to upset Angelina in her fragile state.

"No, I am going to Father Patrick's funeral, and I am going to get up and speak. He was my friend." She began to cry. "I am going and that is that."

They all went to the funeral, and Angelina got up and talked. She was a mess, but she stood up there, and she spoke.

"Hello, everyone, I am Angelina Heart, and Father Patrick was my friend through my whole life. He taught me so many things. He was always there for me through times of joy and times of heartache I could always count on Father Patrick. Today, I stand up here, and I feel sorry for me, because I will miss my friend. This community will miss an amazing priest. But I am happy for Father Patrick. He told me that day he died that he was happy with his life. He knew he was going to heaven and that everything would be perfect there. He told me he was not afraid to die because we only leave our bodies behind when God calls us home. Father Patrick is happy right now. So when you cry, don't cry for him. Because he is in the best place anyone could ever be in, with more love than humanly possible. When I think of Father Patrick, I won't think about how he died or how sad I am. I will think of who he was as a person and all the good things he did for so many people," she spoke then wiped her tears away and took a deep breath.

"I love you, Father Patrick, and I hope you enjoy your new home," she said as she looked up to the ceiling of the church, like she was looking up to heaven, and she blew him a kiss.

After the funeral, everyone came back to Angelina's house, but she just lied in her bed. Harrison came in and laid down with her and held her.

"I am really proud of you. I don't know where you had the strength to get up there today. You always seem to amaze me." Harrison said.

"We do what we have to do, you find strength within yourself when you need it," Angelina said.

"How are you feeling now? I have been really worried about you." Harrison asked.

"I am sorry for worrying you. I guess I am just having a hard time dealing with everything. I know that I sound crazy, but I think when I died, it changed me. I think that maybe I am supposed to help people pass on. I have been helping people through the grieving process but I think, I need to do more." Angelina said. Harrison was scared and didn't really know what to think.

"You do whatever you feel you have to do, and I'll always support you," he said as he hugged her tightly, and then, she started crying again really hard, and he cried with her until she fell asleep.

Angelina spent the next few days, hanging around the house. She was emotional but Harrison was there to comfort her. She woke up from a nap one afternoon, and he was sitting on the bed, looking at her.

"Father Patrick is gone, and I miss him so much, and now he can't marry us, and everything is ruined." She could barely get the words out. She was crying so hard. He wiped her face and looked into her eyes.

"We can do whatever you want to do, but here is an option we can keep everything the same, and Father Brian can marry us, or we can cancel the wedding for now," he said.

"Cancel? I know you would think I am crazy," she said crying.

"No, that's not what I meant. Canceling was the wrong word. I meant postpone. I still love you, and I don't think you are crazy."

"I don't want to cancel the wedding, but I don't want father Brian to marry us either," she said, with her sad eyes looking at him.

"Another option is we could go to Hawaii and get married down there with just the family, and when we get back, we could still have the reception part that has been planned, later. We could do that, or anything you want to do," he said, gently moving her hair out of her face.

"You really love me that much. You would do anything to make me happy, wouldn't you?" she smiled with tears in her eyes.

"Anything," he said. Angelina looked in his eyes and then kissed him.

"I can't get married here at St. Mary's church without Father Patrick. It just would not feel right to me. So yes, I would like to get married in Hawaii with just the family, simple and sweet. But how can we cancel on everyone? That wouldn't be very nice." Angelina said.

"I'll take care of everything, but if you like we can have people over tomorrow night for dinner, and we can tell them together. They'll understand," Harrison said confidently.

After Angelina and Harrison talked, she felt better. The next day, she got up, had a shower, got dressed, did her hair, cleaned the house, and made dinner for everyone.

Harrison just stayed out of her way. She was having a hard time in life, and he didn't want to say anything to set her off, anything was better than her crying and sleeping all the time.

Everyone was sitting at the dining room table, having dinner and talking. After dinner everyone was sitting in the family room and Harrison made the announcement.

"We want to thank you all for coming today. Father Patrick was a great man, and this has been very hard on Angelina and on all of us. We feel we can't get married at St. Mary's church without Father Patrick. So we have decided that we are going to Hawaii and we get married down there. For those of you who want to come, we would love for you to be there. For those of you who can't come, we will still be having a reception when we are back. I hope you all understand and we are sorry for the change of plans, but this is what we want to do," Harrison said, looking around the room at his friends and family, hoping everyone understood.

"That's a great idea," said Henry.

"That's a very expensive idea," said Matt.

"Are you happy with this idea?" Eva asked Angelina, who was just sitting there, not talking.

"Yes, this is what I want to do. I am so sorry, but I really wanted Father Patrick to marry us and now that he can't, I don't really want the big church wedding. Just a simple wedding on the beach with a few of us sounds perfect to me," she said looking at Eva.

"Well, as long as you are happy, I am happy too. I think we can make it work," Eva said. She was still worried about Angelina's mental state.

After everyone left, Henry and Harrison called travel agents to figure out the wedding stuff, and Eva and Angelina cleaned up the house. Henry canceled their trip to Cuba. They booked their wedding and the trip, all in one night on the computer.

CHAPTER 17

After the loss of Father Patrick, Angelina took some time off from work to figure herself out. She started volunteering at the hospital, visiting and talking with the terminally ill. She would just sit and talk to the people that wanted a friend, and she would just pray for the others. Everyone at the hospital called her "the Angel" and some of the nurses and doctors remembered her from when she died and came back to life.

It was a Wednesday, and she was at the hospital, visiting a funny old man named Charlie. He was always cracking jokes. Charlie was a big heavy man, built like a football player, back in the day he played college ball. He was a red neck and had a very strong accent, which only made him funnier. He was bald and had little green eyes.

"Hello, Charlie, can I come visit you today?" she asked him standing in the door way of his hospital room. He was shimmering, so she knew he was the one that would need her that day.

"Oh no. Is it my turn?" he said, looking away from her, trying to be funny.

"What do you mean?" she asked as she walked in to his room and got closer to him.

"Everyone you visit dies after you leave, and I am OK with dying, but, girly, I'm not ready to die today."

"It's not up to me, when it's a person's time to go. I just like visiting people, so they are not alone when their time does come," she said, helping him fix his pillow. "But if you would rather me leave and you all by yourself, I will go."

"Well, no, I don't want you to leave. Stay. Tell me a story, something good," he said, crossing his arms and looking at her with his little green eyes.

"OK, I'll tell you a story, my story, but I have just one question first. Are you afraid to die?" she asked, her voice was clear and sharp. Charlie just looked at her and then a tear came to his eye.

"I am not scared, silly girl, I just don't know what happens next. What if there's nothing? I am not ready to go yet anyway, because I am waiting for my son to come. I know they tell me he is not coming, but I haven't lost faith in him yet. Then I can die even if there is nothing after this life. I just need to say good-bye first." Angelina felt his sadness as she listened to him speak.

She told him her story. When she was done, a nurse came in to check on Charlie. "This girl just told me she died and went to heaven and then came back to life, do you believe that?" he asked the nurse, and she smiled.

"Yes, I believe her, because I worked on her the night she came into the hospital. I was here. I do believe. Yes, I do."

The man just looked at Angelina. He had so much hope in his eyes. Now he lit up with hope and joy.

"So I am going to go to heaven?" His voice was full of excitement. "It's for real that there is more than just this?"

"There is so much more, and I only saw a glimpse of how amazing it is, but the love and joy I felt will stay with me always."

"Do you know when it's going to happen?" he asked her with worry in his voice.

"No, I just don't, but I can feel it's coming soon, but I don't want anyone to be scared or alone." Angelina said.

"It's coming soon. I can feel it, too, and it's not scary. But I'm not going to see my son, am I?" he asked with a tear falling down his face.

Angelina held his hand and looked into his eyes. "I don't know, but I am here now, with you. I am sorry I wish I could do more."

A young man came into the room. He froze and just looked at Charlie, and tears fell down his face.

"Hello, Dad."

Charlie started crying. Angelina left the room and just stood by the door, within ten minutes, a nurse ran into the room. Charlie had died. The young man came out of the room and just stood there, looking at Angelina.

"How did you know my father?" he asked as tears ran down his face.

"I was his friend. I visit the terminally ill here, at the hospital. I just talk to them and befriend them so they are not alone before they go." She said as her voice cracked, she was trying to hold back her own emotions.

"My father told me to talk to you. He told me you were his guardian Angel. He lost his faith a long time ago, and you helped him bring it back," the man said.

"I am glad that he felt that way. I am so glad you came he has been hanging on to see you. I do grief counseling," she said, handing him her card. "Here is my card if you ever want to talk. It's free. Everyone needs someone to talk to sometimes." She was nervous and kept her head down.

The man took her card and shook her hand, and then gave her a hug. She could see that he just needed someone to hug him. "Thank you for telling me that, it means a lot to him that I was here. We didn't always have the best relationship, but he was the only dad I had," he said crying. "Thank you for helping him find his way."

Angelina was walking down the hallway, getting ready to leave the hospital, and she saw a young girl sitting on the ground, crying. When she got closer to her the girl lifted her head. Angelina saw that it was the older Clinton girl (Amy) from the family she counseled.

"Hello, Ms. Heart, is that you?" Amy asked, as she stood up to talk to her.

"Yes, it's me. You can call me Angelina Amy, what's going on?" Angelina asked.

"It's my dad. He is here. Our time is running out," the words cut into Angelina's heart like a knife. She felt all the pain that the girl standing in front of her felt.

"My dad is dying. We are here, saying our good-byes, and it's so hard to see the strongest man I have ever known lying in that hospital bed helpless." She wiped her tears. "How do people get through this? It's so hard I can only stay in there for a few minutes at a time."

"My mom never leaves his side. I remembered what you said about getting to say everything you wanted to say and that how we are lucky to get to say good-bye. So I wrote my dad a letter, telling him everything I want him to know. I'm just trying to find the strength to read it to him." She burst into tears. Angelina just held her in her arms.

"There is nothing I can say to make this easier, but I am here and I will stay here with you for as long as you need me to." Angelina was trying to hold back her tears. "Do you want to go and get a drink or some food? Maybe after that, you will feel strong enough to see your dad again."

"OK, I'll go get Amber, my sister, she needs to eat, too, and tell my mom we are going with you." Amy said.

Angelina stood at the door and looked inside the room. She saw Mr. Clinton. He was not shimmering yet, so Angelina knew she had some time with the girls. Mrs. Clinton came out into the hallway. She was shaking and could barely breathe.

"I really appreciate you offering to take the girls to go get food, you know, you don't have to do that?" she said while blowing her nose and wiping her face.

"I want to help. If this is all I can do, then I want to do it. I was just here, walking by, and I saw Amy. I just thought that maybe a break would be good for the girls. Maybe when we get back, you could take a break, too. I'm here if you want to talk." Angelina didn't want to push them, but she wanted to help in any way she could.

"Yes, that would be nice. Thank you so much." Mrs. Clinton said.

Angelina took the girls out for dinner to a little restaurant just down the street from the hospital. The walk and fresh air helped them calm down. The girls opened up and talked to Angelina while they ate dinner.

"We had such a good summer. We did things as a family again. We went to Niagara Falls for a week and went to Marineland. No one would have known Dad was sick. We all went on the rollercoaster, and dad was being so funny, cracking jokes. It was the greatest week. I will never forget his crazy face on the rollercoaster," Amber said with a smile and tears in her eyes.

"That's a nice memory that you will always have," Angelina said, touching Amber's hand.

"My favorite day this summer was when we rented a cottage up north for a week. It was so much fun. But one day, dad and I went out on the boat, and took it to the middle of the lake and just sat there together in silence. We didn't have to speak. It was just a perfect moment. He was so happy, out there at the cottage, at peace, he loved nature. I loved just being there with him. I would give anything to just be with him on that boat right now." She smiled as tears ran down her face, and she looked at Angelina. "What's the best thing we can do for him now?" Amy asked so seriously. She was so scared. It broke Angelina's heart that these young girls had to go through this.

"Well, he is your dad. He is a man. He wants to take care of you and make sure you are going to be all right. So I would let him know that you will be OK, even if it doesn't feel that way right now. He needs to know that you both will be all right. It might make him feel better to hear that in your own words," Angelina spoke.

They all talked for a few hours, and then they went back to see their dad. They brought Mrs. Clinton a coffee and a sandwich. When they got back to the room, Angelina could see that Mr. Clinton was shimmering, and she knew there wasn't much time left, maybe hours, but only a few.

"Can I say a good-bye just before you girls do?" Angelina asked.

"Yes, of course," Mrs. Clinton said, hugging her girls. "The three of us could use a minute together."

Angelina walked into the room and looked at the man lying in the bed. He didn't look like the same man she had met just a few months ago. "Mr. Clinton, I wanted to tell you something. You don't have to be scared to die. You are going to a beautiful place, where everything is perfect. You will be happy there. I know that heaven exists because I have seen it, and I saw the beauty that lives there. God is calling you home now. You have to hold on just for a little bit longer, your two amazing daughters need to say good-bye to you. I want you to know I will be here and do whatever I can to help support them after you are gone. I want you to know that somehow they will be OK. They still have each other," she said, wiping her tears.

"I know you will take care of them because you are an Angel. I can see your glowing blue eyes, and I can see your halo," Mr. Clinton spoke in a very low raspy voice with a smile on his face.

Angelina went into the hallway to talk to the girls. "Amy and Amber, if you have anything you want to say to your dad, say it right now, don't hold anything back. Amy read your letter to him now." The girls went into the room one at a time to talk to their father. Amber went in first and came out with tears pouring down her face and she fell into her mother's arms. Amy went in next.

Angelina stood outside of the room and talked to Mrs. Clinton as she held Amber in her arms. They could here Amy reading her letter to dad. It was heart breaking.

"Can I talk to you privately for one minute?" Angelina asked Mrs. Clinton. They walked away from Amber for a moment.

"Do you want the girls to be here when it happens? Because I don't know how to explain, how I know this, but it's going to happen soon, really soon, maybe within hours. Do you have family you could call? I can take the girls home and stay with them until someone can come and be with them. Or I can stay here with you, whatever you want. But I want you to know you need to say good-bye next, because it's coming." Angelina was so scared that she was going to yell at her or think she was crazy, but she didn't.

"OK, I will say good-bye. I will ask the girls, what they want to do, and if you will take them home, that would be nice. Thank you for all your help. It is greatly appreciated."

"I just want to help. Is there anything I can do for you?" she asked Mrs. Clinton.

Mrs. Clinton started shaking and crying hysterically. She couldn't control herself.

"Me? What about me? I don't know how to do this. What? Watch him die and then go home and sleep in our bed and raise our children all by myself? This wasn't the plan. We were supposed to go together in our sleep when we were ninety." She let out a little laugh. "I don't know how to grieve myself and be there for everyone else. I don't think I am strong enough to get through this." She cried.

"You are an incredible woman, terrific mother, and an amazing wife. You love your family more than anything in this world. No matter how bad things get, you will find strength within you to get through all of this. You will get through this, because you have to. Those two girls need you, and you need them even more. You will support each other through this. It's going to be the hardest experience any of you ever go through, but it will only make you stronger, better, and bring you closer.

Your husband loves you, and all he wants is to know you will be OK, and I know you will, because you have each other," Angelina spoke as she held Mrs. Clinton in her arms.

"Thank you. I think I needed to hear how incredible I am." She said letting out a little laugh and wiping her face.

Amy walked out of the room and she fell on the ground and cried. Her mother picked her up and held her for a long time.

"Do you want to be here when it happens or do you want to go home? Angelina has offered to take you both home and stay with you until Grandma can get there. I will stay and call Uncle Nick to come be with me, and I will call you when it happens, or if you want to be here that is your choice." Mrs. Clinton asked the girls with tears in her eyes, and she held both her girls in her arms.

"No, I can't stay. I can't watch him die. That can't be my last memory of my father. I want to go home and stay with Angelina,"

Amy said, putting her hand to her mouth, like she was shocked by her decision to leave.

"Yes, I want to go, too. I don't want to watch my dad die," Amber said, crying. Amy put her arm over her sister and hugged her real tight.

"You are not alone. I will always be here with you. I am glad you are my sister."

The three of them went into the room to say good-bye as a family.

Mrs. Clinton gave Angelina directions on how to get to their house and told the girls to call Grandma. Angelina took the girls home, and they all sat on the couch and talked.

They were there for about two hours, when the phone rang. Both girls stopped talking. Angelina answered the phone. She held the phone to her ear and a tear fell down her cheeks. The two girls held each other and cried. Angelina hung up the phone and sat on the couch beside the girls.

"He died, didn't he?" Amy asked, already knowing the answer.

Angelina shook her head yes. "Your mom and Uncle Nick will be coming home soon. She said some family and friends are on their way over to be with you. But I'll stay or go whatever you need." Angelina sat on the couch and hugged the girls. As emotional as she was she did her best to be strong for the girls.

The doorbell rang, and before they knew it, the house was

full of people. Angelina was making coffee and serving people food. The girls sat in the living room, telling stories about their dad. Mrs. Clinton came home. Angelina gave her a hug, and Mrs. Clinton held her really tight.

"Angelina, I can't believe you are still here. Thank you so much for taking care of my girls. How are they?" She asked with this hopeless look in her eyes.

"They have their moments, but they are doing well. They are talking about their dad, remembering him and how great he was. I couldn't leave without making sure you were OK. If there is anything you need, just let me know," Angelina said, putting on her coat as she was getting ready to leave.

"Right now, I don't know how I am feeling, and I don't know how I am even walking, but thank you so much. I don't think we need anything, but I am sure we will come soon to talk to you. Things are going to get harder before they get easier," Mrs. Clinton replied.

"OK, well, I am going to go and let your family deal with things. But I will be here if you need me, really. I am not saying that just to be nice, honestly, I will be here. Just call." Angelina walked out the front door of the Clinton house, when Amy came running after her.

"Angelina, wait," she screamed. She ran up to her and threw her arms around Angelina. Tears were pouring out of her eyes. She could barely see.

"My dad died. Oh my god, my dad died." Angelina just held

her for a long time and let her cry. "Thank you for being here today, it's nice to have someone to talk to who isn't family," Amy said.

"Here is my card with my home number. Call me if you want to talk or even hang out, just as friends, anything you need," she said, hugging Amy.

When Angelina got home, it was 10:30 p.m., and Harrison was sitting on the couch. He looked worried and mad. She walked into the living room and started crying and fell into his arms.

"I am so sorry. I didn't call I was at the hospital all day. I helped a family I knew. Their dad died today, so I took the kids home. I spent the whole day helping the family," Angelina said. "I am so sorry, and I am so tired. Can we just go to bed?"

Harrison wrapped his arms around her body, looked into her eyes, and touched her face.

"You are amazing, and I love you. Let's go to bed," he said as he kissed her forehead, and they walked up the stairs.

A few days later, Angelina and Harrison went to the funeral of Mr. Clinton. Angelina continued to help the girls. She would go visit the family once a week. They would all talk together, and then she spent some one-on-one time with each of them. Amy became very close to Angelina. They would hang out and go to the movies and out for lunch. It was nice for both of them.

CHAPTER 18

Things were right on track. Angelina was helping people and still public speaking and volunteering at the hospital one-day-a-week. The wedding was coming up, and everyone was excited about going to Hawaii. A couple of weeks before, they left to go on their trip, Angelina was doing a group counseling session with a class Dina Hayford taught. They were discussing how drugs can alter the choices you make. It turned into a debate. Angelina enjoyed working with the group; it was fun and different for her.

When Angelina was leaving the college, Dina Hayford introduced her to Johanna Bing and Max Norman. They worked for the Catholic school board. They were interested in Angelina visiting high schools as an inspirational speaker and talked about her experiences and educating the kids on gangs and drugs. Angelina agreed. They scheduled her for four dates at different schools in the Toronto area.

Harrison got an offer for a full-time job at the drug and alcohol counseling center.

Matthew and Gwen moved into the apartment. Angelina and Harrison liked having friends around. Gwen and Angelina were becoming pretty close because they were together all the time, but it was nice for her to have a girlfriend that was close to her own age.

Finally the day had come. They were all going to Hawaii. Everyone was meeting at Angelina and Harrison's house, and a limo was coming to take them to the airport. Everyone was really tired, because it was 2:00 a.m., the twins were sleeping on the couch, and Eva and Henry were bringing everything they needed into the house. Henry's parents and his sister Wendy and her husband, Gary, showed up with more luggage than most people ever own.

Matt and Gwen fell asleep on the couch with the twins. Angelina and Harrison allowed Matt to not pay rent for a few months so they could afford to go on the trip with them and so they could be there for their wedding.

Eva's best friend Helen and her husband, Joe, showed up just as the limo came. Everyone met and shook hands. Everyone was so tired but so excited.

"Is this everyone that is coming?" Henry asked.

"This is everyone that is coming with us, but Dina Hayford and her husband, Ken, are already down in Hawaii. They had the trip book a long time ago, and it just worked out and they'll be at the wedding. My old boss Maria from the women's shelter and her daughter Olivia are coming down on Monday so they will be there for the wedding as well," Angelina told him. She was so excited that she was clapping her hands with joy.

Everyone packed up and got into the limo, then everyone one cheered "Hawaii!" They waited at the airport for a long time before they boarded the plane. The twins were so good. They slept for the whole plane ride to Hawaii.

Angelina looked over at Harrison, who was holding on to the arm rest for dear life. He was shaking and sweating. He was so nervous about flying. He hadn't been on a plane since his parents died. She touched him and gently rubbed his arm and then she kissed the palm of his hand.

"You have nothing to worry about, not one person on this plane is going to die today. Trust me, I know," she said, winking at him trying to be cute and funny.

"You know, you're really cute, I can't help being nervous, but thanks, it helps to know that we are not going to die," he said, letting out a little nervous laugh.

Angelina had a window seat on the plane. She had never been on a plane before. She had never done a lot of things until she was with Harrison. She wasn't nervous at all. She was content and had this warm happy feeling all over her body. She just looked out the window into the clouds and she did believe that her parents were there, looking at her. She believed that they were proud and happy for her, that she had found someone to love and someone who makes her so happy. Looking in the clouds, she thought about heaven. There were moments almost every day that she missed the beauty and perfect happiness and love of that place. But as soon Harrison touched her hand or looked at her with his loving big brown eyes, she knew earth was where she was meant to be right now, with him.

He touched her hand and looked at her. He saw a tear ran down her cheek, and he wiped it away. His touch made her heart glow with love and joy. She loved him so much.

"Are you nervous?" he whispered.

"No, not at all. I am so ready to marry you. I was just having a moment thinking about my parents," she whispered and sent him a sweet innocent smile.

"I understand. I have been thinking about my parents a lot lately. It's hard to believe they are not here for this," he said, squeezing her hand "I think we should do something special to include them in the wedding."

"Yes, that would be nice so we could feel like they are a part of our celebration," she said.

When they got to the resort, it was 3:00 p.m. everyone was so tired that they all split away and went to their rooms. Harrison and Angelina walked through the resort to get to their room. The resort was so beautiful. The sun was beaming down on them, and the trees were moving in the wind. The palm trees were so beautiful, and there were flowers everywhere in so many different colors. The resort was large but had a nice layout so it was easy to find their way to their room.

Harrison and Angelina walked into the room, and they stopped and looked in amazement.

"Wow! this is lovely." Angelina was amazed. It was all so beautiful. They had a whole suite to themselves, not just a room. They walked into the sitting room. The walls were white, but there was so much color in the room from other things. The couches were of black leather, and they had pillows of all different colors—blue, red, yellow, and purple. There was a coffee table with fresh cut flowers in a vase. A big flat-screen TV was mounted on the wall. Behind the couch was a dark wood dining room table. They had three vases sitting on the table, all with fresh cut flowers—red and blue ones—it was all so beautiful. The room was so colorful. The artwork on the walls and the curtains on the windows were very colorful, too. Then they walked into the bedroom. It was so amazing. The room was white; the furniture was a dark cherry wood. The bed was a king size canapé bed; that had purple sheer curtains hanging off of it. Fresh cut purple flowers were on the dresser. Two side tables on both side of the bed were there, and they had black lamps with a purple shade on them. On the other side of the room, in the corner, was a big Jacuzzi tub. Big French doors lead outside to a deck, it was so incredible. A table and some chairs sat on the deck and a there was a hemic big enough for two. After checking out the whole suite, they both sat down on the couch. She fell into his arms.

"This place is so beautiful. Thank you for bringing me here. I am so excited to be here. I'm so tired, but I can't sleep. I just want to explore this amazing place," she said looking at him with her big eyes glowing with excitement, hoping he wanted to explore the resort, too.

"I know this place is so beautiful. OK, well, why don't we change into cooler clothes and go exploring. Maybe, we will find a place to eat. I'm so hungry." Harrison changed into shorts and a t-shirt, and Angelina put on a blue summer dress, just as they were going to leave, there was a knock at the door. When they opened the door, there was a little lady standing there.

"Aloha! You two must be Harrison and Angelina." She had a very strong accent, but they could understand everything she was saying as they shook her hand.

"I am Minima. I am your wedding coordinator and your travel hostess, so if you need anything, you come to me. I hope you are happy with your suite. All your guests are just in the next plaza over. You are special guests, so you get the suite. Here is your package. She handed Harrison a big red envelope. You two have fun today, enjoy yourselves. Tomorrow, we meet at 4:00 p.m. and go through all the plans for your wedding. But one more thing, tonight, I have reserved dinner for your party at the Luna beach restaurant. Its right on the beach about 8:00 p.m., and then, right after that, there is a great show in the main bar. You have to see the shows. They are the best. Well, do you have any questions right now before I leave you?"

"Is there a place we can go eat right now? We are so hungry," Harrison asked.

"Yes, right past the main lobby is a bar area. You can eat in there; they have food all the time and there is a lunch hut on the beach as well,"

"Thank you. We'll see you tomorrow."

They left their room and went to find the others. Most of their guests went to have a nap. So Harrison, Mathew, Gwen, and Angelina went to go eat and explore. After they ate, they walked all over the resort. It was so amazing. They walked up and down the beach and walked over to some big rocks.

"This will be beautiful for wedding photos," Harrison said, smiling at her.

"Wow! I can't believe we are getting married here. I think this is the most beautiful place on earth. I am so happy," she said as she walked over to Harrison and gave him a big hug. "I love you." She kissed him as they were standing on a big rock. A big wave washed over them. They ended up getting soaked. Everyone laughed, and they all ran back to their rooms.

Everyone got all dressed up for the dinner at the beach restaurant. It was cute, because all the girls were wearing black dresses except for Angelina. She was wearing a cream-colored knit dress with a matching headband and matching shoes. When they got to the restaurant, Dina and Ken Hayford were there, waiting for them.

Dina looked like she got a makeover. She got her hair dyed with brown and blonde highlights, and she cut her hair short to her chin. It looked so good. Dina ran over to Angelina and gave her a hug.

"You look beautiful. This place is amazing. You are going to love it here, this is my husband Ken," Dina said and introduced them. Angelina shook Ken's hand.

"It's so nice to finally meet the famous Angelina. My wife thinks the world of you. She talks about you all the time," Ken said. He was a short, stocky man with thinning golden hair and hazel eyes. He had bushy eyebrows and a beard hiding most of his face.

"I think the world of her, too. She had been a good friend to me this year, and this is my soon-to-be husband Harrison," Angelina said smiling and introducing them to each other.

Everyone got acquainted, and then they all went to sit down at the table. The twins, Lilly and Josh, were so happy. They kept singing "It's party time, it's so much fun." They all had a really nice dinner. Everyone talked and got to know each other.

"I just like to say, Angelina and Harrison, we are all so happy to be here with you in the most beautiful place. We all love you." Henry said as he lifted his glass. "Here's to good times, happy memories, a beautiful wedding, and one hell of a vacation,"

After dinner, they went to watch the show; they had professional hula dancers on stage. They put on a great show. After that, they called all the children up on stage to teach them a dance. Lilly was so happy. Josh was a little shy, but they were so cute on stage trying to perform hula.

The host of the show was a dark man wearing a red suit. He

called himself Gayu. He called on stage all the couples getting married in Hawaii that week.

Angelina was so embarrassed. Her whole face was red. There were two other couples on stage. The man asked all three couples where they were from and how long they had been together.

"I think we need to have a competition to see who is going to be, Hawaii's no. 1 couple of the week." Gayu said.

They made all three girls leave the stage, and the guys were told that when the girls come back, they have to play and sing them a love song. There was a bunch of instruments. They had the choice of bongos, a ukulele, guitar, bamboo flute, or maracas.

Harrison took the guitar. One guy took the bongos, and the last guy took the ukulele. When the girls came back on stage, they were wearing hula dancer outfits. All the girls sat down on chairs.

Each guy had their turn doing a love song. The first two guys took the funny route by singing kids songs. It was Harrison's turn. He picked up the guitar and stood in front of the microphone and looked right into Angelina's eyes.

"I only know how to play one song, and I haven't played it since high school, My dad taught it to me, I hope you like it. He started playing the guitar, the melody was slow and soft.

I didn't release I was lost and couldn't find my way back home.

I didn't know I was broken until I found you, and you taught me how to be happy and live life and love someone so much.

I didn't know what love was until I found you and I just want to say thank you.

You the reason that I try so hard, you the reason for the smile on my face you're the reason that I am so happy today and you're the reason I know what love is.

Even though Harrison wasn't the best singer, he did a great job. He had everyone in the audience clapping.

Angelina had tears in her eyes. He was so cute. She got up from her chair to kiss him. After the guys were done, it was the girls' turn. Each guy sat on a chair.

The girls had to do their best creative hula dance with hula hoops; each girl had five hula hoops. The goal was to use all five in their dance. Each girl did something a little different. One girl did a sexy dance and put the hula hoops around her man, and the other girl put all the hula hoops around on her waist.

Angelina started hauling and then she added one hula hoop to her waist and then two more to her waist. Angelina put the last two hula hoops on each of her arm while still dancing.

Everyone cheered for Angelina and Harrison. Their performances were so much fun. They won the no. 1 couple award of Hawaii.

"I can't believe we just own that," Angelina said walking off the stage and laughing. "I loved that song; I have never heard it before,"

"That was so much fun, my dad wrote that song for my mom and when I was in high school he was teaching me how to play. But that was the only song I learned before he passed away, after that I didn't really care about playing so I never learn any other songs," Harrison said looking into her eyes. They walked over to their friends and family.

"You two were awesome, I have the whole thing on video," Dina said laughing, holding up her video camera.

Everyone had so much fun. They all had some drinks and danced and explored the resort as a bid group. Eva was taking lots of pictures, she wanted to have lots of memories of the beautiful place.

CHAPTER 19

Everyone spent the next day at the beach. Harrison and Angelina went and met with the wedding coordinator. They made all the plans for their wedding. The next few days were so much fun. Everyone stayed together and explored and had fun as a group, spending most of the time in the water by the pool or in the ocean.

The night before the wedding, Eva and the other girls decided that Harrison and Angelina couldn't see each other on the night before the wedding. So that night was girls' and boys' night out alone, one last single night out. The girls got all dressed up and went out for dinner, just the girls, and the boys did the same thing at a different restaurant. The girls went to one bar, and the boys went to another bar. They danced and had some drinks and had a good time. The girls went back to Angelina's room for the night. They did manicures and pedicures on each other. The guys stayed up late in Matthew's room. They had some drinks and just talked.

"Man, I can't believe you're getting married tomorrow. Are you nervous that this has all happened so fast?" Matt asked.

"I am not nervous at all. I can't wait to be married to Angelina. She is amazing. I am so happy, and I have no worries or doubts. I honestly believe things happen for a reason. I want to spend the rest of my life with her. I think that's when you know it's right. When you don't ever want to be with anyone else," replied Harrison.

"I am happy for you, but Gwen and I have been together for way longer than the two of you, and I am not ready for marriage at all," Matt said, shaking his head.

"And that's OK, because you know what's right for you, and I know what's right for me. I am also four years older than you. So that makes a difference. I am ready to settle down and start a family." Harrison said.

"Have a family?" Matt made a funny face. "Angelina is pregnant, isn't she?"

"No, Matt, honestly, she is not pregnant. I just meant that someday soon, I would like to have kids." Harrison shook his head and took another drink.

The next day, all the girls got breakfast brought to their room. There was French toast, Belgium waffles, fruit, and coffee, tea, and juice. All the girls were getting ready. They went down to the spa in the hotel and got their hair and makeup done.

The guys spent most of the day down by the pool. Until

it was time to get ready, Harrison was wearing a very simple outfit—light khaki dress pants and ivory polo shirt, and Matt was wearing khaki pants with a dark blue polo shirt. Henry was wearing black dress pants and dress shirt, and his son Josh was wearing the cutest little short tuxedo it was adorable.

Eva was wearing her pretty blue dress with blue flip-flops. She had her hair all up in curls. Lilly was wearing a very pretty flower girl dress that had a blue sash across the waist, and her pretty blonde hair was pinned up in curls. Eva went into the bathroom to get Angelina into her dress.

Angelina slipped into her dress, and Eva did it up for her and tied the blue sash around her waist. She slipped her feet into her blue shoes, and she was already to go. Eva just looked at her with tears in her eyes. Her beauty was breathtaking.

"Wow, I am so proud to stand by your side today. I feel like the mother of the bride," Eva said, blowing her nose.

"You are my mom in every sense of the word. You have taken care of me, you raised me, and you have always been there no matter what. You know everything about me. You are my best friend, my aunt, my family. I am so happy you are here with me today. I know my parents are happy that you are with me, and they would be so grateful to you for raising their little girl. I have become who I am because of you. I love you so much." Angelina was emotional but she was trying not to cry she didn't want to ruin her make up. They stood there and hugged for a few minutes.

They both came out of the bathroom, and all the girls stared at Angelina. She was worried when no one spoke.

"Wow, you look perfect," Lilly said while giggling. "You are the most beautiful Angel ever."

"Thank you, Lilly, you look beautiful too. Are you sure I look OK?" Angelina asked looking at the others for approval.

"Shut up, you are so beautiful," Gwen said pushing Angelina in front of a body length mirror. "Look at yourself. You look amazing. Don't tell me it's not true,"

Angelina saw herself fully for the first time. Some of her hair was pinned up in curls but most of it was down. She had curls cascading down her back. It was really nice but simple at the same time. She didn't wear her blue crystal headband, instead they put a pretty blue flower in her hair. That worked better for a beach wedding. Her dress was as beautiful as she remembered it to be. It could not have been more perfect for her. The off-white lace was perfect for her skin tone, and the cap sleeve square neckline suited the shape of her neck and shoulders. It showed off her shape because it fit to her body. The short length was perfect as she had nice legs to show off. In the back it went longer like a short train so that it still looked like a wedding dress. It was simple but classic just like her. She stood there looking at herself in the mirror and tears came to her eyes. She had never seen it before that moment but she looked like her mother. She had to admit she looked beautiful.

There was a knock at the door , Angelina was hiding she didn't want anyone to see her yet.

"Are you girls beautiful yet because your chariot awaits?" Henry said smiling as he was peeking into the room.

Everyone left to go to the ceremony site. Eva, Henry, and the twins were going with Angelina; a limo golf cart came to pick them up. When Angelina walked out, Henry started to get emotional he was chocking back his tears.

"You truly are an Angel because I don't think humans are as beautiful as you are today," Henry said in a deep clear voice, as he looked into her eyes.

She gave him a big hug and kissed his cheek. "Thank you," she said with the biggest smile on her face.

They arrived at the ceremony site. They got out of the limo cart and stepped onto the beach. There was a big long dock that went out into the ocean. They stepped onto the dock and a man started playing guitar. Lilly and Josh walked up the dock, then Eva made her way up the dock.

Henry took hold of Angelina's arm and she wasn't shaking or nervous at all she was in complete control.

"Shall I give you a way to this man who loves you so much?" Henry said looking down at her glowing face. She was beaming with happiness and she just smiled.

"Yes please, I am ready now," she spoke so sweet and softly.

They started walking. It was beautiful. At the end of the dock was a round look out point that had a roof. It was perfect. They had a blue runner between the chairs the guests sat on. They had blue lanterns hanging from the roof and blue, red, and white flowers everywhere. It was so simple but so beautiful. It wasn't a wedding on a beach, it was right above the sea and just below the clouds. As they got close, her eyes met his, and they both had tears falling down their cheeks. They got to where Harrison was standing and he held out his hand for hers and she reached for him. Standing face-to-face they both had the biggest smiles. Their happiness was shining out of both of them. They both said their vows they had written together. They both cried through the whole ceremony. It was very beautiful.

"I give you my heart. I give myself to you today. I promise to love you always. I promise to be your partner in life. I will always support you. I trust you and respect you. I will laugh with you and cry with you. I will lean on you and I will be there for you to lean on through good times and bad. Regardless of what we may face together, we will get through anything. I give you my hand, my heart, my love from this day always."

"I now pronounce you husband and wife, you may kiss your bride," the minister said.

Harrison looked into her eyes and pulled her close to him. His lips touched hers and her lips kissed his back. After the ceremony, they went to take photos all over the resort.

The dinner and reception was in a private restaurant on the beach. It was so beautiful. They had set up tables with blue tablecloths and chairs with white covers on them. There were candles burning on each table and they had blue and white lanterns with lights in them hanging all over the place. It was simple and elegant.

Dinner was really good. Everyone got up to say a few words.

"We are so grateful for all of you for coming here to celebrate with us. Today has been more amazing than anyone could ask for. We couldn't be happier," Harrison said. After thanking his guests, he held Angelina's hand and looked into her eyes.

"Thank you for becoming my wife, my love, and my partner. I am so happy to share my life with you. I hope I always make you as happy as you make me. I would do anything for you. I want our life to be happy together. It's so crazy to think a year ago I was just some bachelor college student renting an apartment from my aunt and now I have a career, own a beautiful home, and I am married to the most amazing woman I have ever met." Harrison held up his glass. "To my angel, I am so happy you came back to me. I love you with all my heart," he said and bent down and kissed her.

Then Angelina spoke shaking with excitement.

"Thank you all for being here and for your support. We really appreciate it. To my aunt and uncle, we both love you so much. We can never thank you enough for everything you have done for us. To think back at the last year, I had no life. I really didn't have many friends, I just went to school and worked and spent all my free time with my nose in a book or at church. I never really realized how lonely I was until now. Having people around all the time is so nice. I never really let people in because I was afraid to lose them. But now I understand that it's better to love, really love, and be so happy even if it's just for a little while than to never know what that feels like. It's so nice to know we will always have each other to depend on," she said looking at Harrison smiling at her. "Thank you, Harrison, for opening me up to this whole new world of living, being happy, feeling loved, having friends, traveling. I wouldn't be who I am now if it wasn't for you. I love so much and I am so happy to have you as my partner, my love, my family."

"Kiss, kiss, kiss!" everyone chanted.

Harrison pulled Angelina into his arms. His lips touched hers and she kissed him back. It was time for their first dance as husband and wife. The wedding coordinator had a dance area all set up with lights. The doors were open so they could see the ocean rolling in on the beach. They danced to "A perfect moment."

It was so amazing; everything was the way Angelina wanted it to be. Everyone danced and had a good time. Angelina and Harrison had something special they wanted to do at midnight. Everyone walked out to the beach. There was a band playing music and ladies handing out sparklers and light lanterns. Harrison and Angelina put letters into a bottle and corked it. They sent out their letters in a bottle out to sea. As they did that, their guests had sparklers burning and they let the lanterns go. Everyone together said a little prayer and went back to the party.

Harrison pulled Angelina onto the dance floor and she wrapped her arms around his neck.

"So it's just you and me now," he said, his face glowing with happiness and he looked into her eyes.

"Let our journey begin," she said smiling as she pulled his head down to reach hers and she placed her lips on his lips and they shared a kiss.

MESSAGE IN A BOTTLE

Dear Mom and Dad,

Today was my wedding day. I married the most amazing girl I have ever met. I know you both would love her. Being with her makes me a better person just because she is so good. She is so genuine and has such a pure heart. I want to do better when I am with her. I wish you could have been here to see how happy I am and to see the man I have become. I think you would be proud of me. I want to thank you for being such good parents to me. I miss you so much and love you always. I used to be mad at God for taking you away from me but now I am grateful that I had at least seventeen years with you. Some people don't even get that long. Now I know how lucky I am. It's so funny how the things that make our lives the hardest are the same things that define who we are as a person and make us stronger and better people. I love you both always.

Love, your son Harrison

Dear Mom and Dad,

Every little girl dreams of her wedding day and how it's going to be, but not me. I didn't think this day would happen to me. I used to feel like I was just invisible, just a person with no purpose in life. Now I have someone who actually sees me, loves me, and thinks the world of me. I have a purpose. I know who I am and I know all the things I want to do in my life before I see you again. It was so special my short time with you both. I always believed you two were in heaven but it was so amazing to see you. I wanted to go be with you in heaven my whole life but when I was there I couldn't stay. A part of me wanted to stay with you but I had so much still left to do in my life. I am so happy I got a glimpse of heaven. I know my story has helped people and my experience has helped me open myself up to new possibilities. I have fallen in love with someone who is perfect for me. He is so understanding and kind. We complement each other so well. We are a perfect match. You too would love him because he is the best, and when I am with him I am better too. I had to die to realize I wasn't living before. Now that I have a second chance at life, I am going to live. I want to be happy. I want to make a difference in this world. I want to experience everything. I am so happy to share my life with my new husband. I know you are always with me, watching over me and guiding me through my life. I know you were watching over us today as we exchanged our marriage vows, but I wish you could have been here today for real to see how truly happy I am for the first time since you both died. I take comfort in knowing I have you both watching over me always, and now that I have a partner in life,

I will never be alone. I love you both with every beat of my heart and I'll know where I am going the next time you see me. When it is my time to go to heaven, I'll be on the staircase to heaven getting my wings. Until we meet again, I'll carry you both with me in my heart always!

Loving you always, your little Angel

Edwards Brothers Malloy
Thorofare, NJ USA
May 25, 2012